The CULT *of*
QUICK REPAIR

The CULT of QUICK REPAIR

Dede CRANE

COTEAU BOOKS

Edited by J. Jill Robinson.
Cover and series design by Duncan Campbell.
Cover photo: "Woman stumbling on red carpet with broken heel, lower section, rear view" by Jason Hetherington, Stone collection/Getty Images.

Printed and bound in Canada at Gauvin Press.
This book is printed on 100% recycled paper.

Library and Archives Canada Cataloguing in Publication

Crane, Dede
The cult of quick repair / Dede Crane.

ISBN 978-1-55050-392-0

I. Title.
PS8605.R35C84 2008   C813'.6   C2008-901472-3

10 9 8 7 6 5 4 3 2 1

2517 Victoria Ave.
Regina, Saskatchewan
Canada   S4P 0T2

AVAILABLE IN CANADA & THE US FROM
Fitzhenry & Whiteside
195 Allstate Parkway
Markham, ON, Canada, L3R 4T8

The publisher gratefully acknowledges the financial assistance of the Saskatchewan Arts Board, the Canada Council for the Arts, the Government of Canada through the Book Publishing Industry Development Program (BPIDP), Association for the Export of Canadian Books, and the City of Regina Arts Commission, for its publishing program.

To Lantz...with a zed

CONTENTS

Seers

EVERY WEDNESDAY, WREN FOREGOES A bagged lunch in the lounge and treats herself to a quiet restaurant meal alone with the morning's paper. The restaurant, Venus Risen, is a converted fifties gas station which sits directly across the street from the ultrasound clinic where Wren works. The restaurant walls and floor are a pearly pink, just like the inside of a conch shell, and cheering on this overcast March day. In an intricate mosaic of tiles, Venus's naked blonde body climbs the middle of one wall. A labour of love is how Wren thinks of it. This Wednesday Shannon, the "single gal" as she's known in the clinic, and by far the most talkative of Wren's co-workers, asked to come along. Wren was unable to say no.

"How was your morning? Thin or thick?" asks Shannon as she drifts pepper over both her potato chips and the bread of a club sandwich.

"Just cons." Wren's never seen someone pepper the outside of a sandwich. She blows on the tomato soup couched in her spoon and orangey red drops spray on the table. "Oh, sorry." She wipes them away with her napkin.

Thick and thin referred to a patient's ultrasound file. Those with thick files were cons – hypochondriacs – meaning people they saw too regularly. The thinner the file, usually, the more serious the problem.

"I had an enlarged gallbladder, kidney stones, and a terminal," says Shannon, wrinkling her nose. Her midlength hair is stylishly layered with copper and bronze highlights. "Course I didn't have to look at his insides to know he was a goner. His skin was the same colour as people in black and white movies." She bites her club sandwich but keeps talking. "He was old at least. Oh," – half-chewed food tumbles behind her teeth – "I haven't told you about last Friday. Lucky Friday."

Shannon's enthusiasm makes Wren feel old. Ten years younger than Wren, Shannon's the type who tells all, assumes (wrongly in Wren's case), that everyone can relate. Wren tries to glean the headline from the newspaper on the table across the aisle.

"Well," Shannon slaps the table, "as you know, Bob was pretty unimaginative. Mechanical you might say. Like he was snaking out the toilet or something."

"Right." Wren drops her eyes to her soup. She didn't know.

"But Ryan..." Shannon's face seems to dilate. "Now he's another story."

A waitress comes and, without asking, tops up their coffee. She has a reddish pink stain on her shirt. Ketchup? Blood?

"Thanks," says Wren, though she didn't really want more.

Shannon waits, bug-eyed, until the waitress leaves. "Okay. First he takes me out to dinner." She says this with a hill-and-valley lilt in her voice, accompanied by an exaggerated nod up then down. "Then we drive to Arbutus Cove with a bottle of wine." Another lilting nod. "He has a blanket in his car..." up and down "...and we find a secluded spot." This time only her eyebrows do the nodding. "And, what can I say." She lowers her voice. "He took his time, got me in positions I wasn't sure I'd be able to get out of." She laughs through her nose.

Wren isn't sure she heard right. They were outside? Isn't that illegal?

"And he made me," she leans in across the table and, despite herself, Wren meets her halfway, "masturbate myself while we were doing it."

"Made you?" Wren tries to sound offhand.

"I just mean he asked me to." Shannon knocks back in her seat. "I know it's no biggie but it *was* our first time and you know how guys want to prove themselves first go, which is sweet, but pretty hit and miss. Or they think their magnificent thing is all it takes. *Helloo.*"

Shannon smirks at Wren and Wren smirks back, hiding her blush behind the steam of her coffee cup, which threatens to cloud the front of her glasses. Her sex life isn't something she shares with people.

Recipes are for sharing. Cold remedies. Greg would be appalled.

"I felt so comfortable around this guy. I've never," another hushed lean-in, "come so many times." Shannon shivers and scrunches up her eyes.

Wren pictures a similar shiver and scrunch with each orgasm. How many? she wants to ask. But enough already.

"So, we'll see where Ryan and I go from here." Shannon leans back in her chair, taps the table with one bronze painted nail. "If nothing else I can say he taught me a thing or...seven." She smiles and pops a whole chip in her mouth. Crunch.

Wren dips her grilled cheese in her soup. "Sounds like he's worth a follow-up."

Seven? She wonders if Shannon is being facetious. Wren has never been able to have more than one at a go. One good one though. At least it feels pretty substantial. How much better do they get? And why ice a cake seven times?

She married Greg, her one and only lover, when she was twenty-four. She'd kept her virginity not for moral or religious reasons, she just never found somebody she trusted until Greg. He was uncomplicated, had a weak chin, was a little shy, like her. Sex naturally seemed to lead to marriage. Seventeen years and two nearly grown kids later, she can't help wondering what a different guy might bring out in a woman. Seven? Good ones? Maybe the first six were more like pleasure rushes, lead-ups to the big seventh. Or maybe it was one big one and six bloopers.

"Any birthday plans?" asks Shannon.

"I think Greg's planning something behind my back," Wren says, grateful for the change of topic. "He threw me one at thirty. Now here comes the big four-o." She eyes Shannon closely, wonders if she's playing dumb and is in on the surprise.

Shannon scans the table. "I'm sure he'll do something nice. Where'd the pepper go? Did that waitress take the pepper?"

Wren slides the pepper from behind a plastic stand advertising Sunday brunch. She contrasts her hand with Shannon's. Her pores gape in comparison, her bulging blue green veins like mountains on a topographical map. Forty. Vicky and James both in high school. And she's been working in ultrasound how long? Is it really twelve years this January? What else has she missed out on besides multiple orgasms?

"I saw that Haspray guy on next week's schedule," says Shannon, starting another triangle of sandwich.

"Who?"

"Tim Haspray. You know, circles under his eyes, insists he's got a hernia. Young. Not bad looking if he wasn't so bizarre. I got him once and I think Pat got him last time. Major con."

"Ponytail?" Wren wears her hair in a ponytail most of the time, in a clip at her neck.

Shannon nods and swallows. "He didn't come on to me or anything, but it's obvious he likes some woman rubbing him down there. Like old Mr. Cowley. 'A little lower, please,'" she mimics in a quavery voice. "How's 'bout more of that warm gel?'" Shannon's tongue lolls out the side of her mouth.

Wren laughs. She wonders if she should get her hair cut, then remembers Greg prefers it long.

"Hey, I'll pay for your lunch if you take ponytail guy," says Shannon.

"Sure, thanks."

Shannon leans forward. "Don't these walls remind you of the inside of a woo-woo?"

SUNDAY IS THEIR MORNING to sleep in, make love, then cook a hearty breakfast together – either eggs Florentine or homemade waffles with fruit and whipped cream – which they eat in the sunroom with Saturday's *Globe & Mail*. The routine's like an old sweater, comforting but well-worn, and Wren wonders if they'll be doing the same at sixty.

Since neither of them has bothered to get up and brush their teeth, they keep their faces averted. It's a sleepy groping, a slow awakening of nerves and senses as Greg snuggles in behind her and his belly presses into her lower back. His stiff beard tickles her shoulder as he slips his hand under her T-shirt to brush her nipples upwards like she once told him she liked, fifteen years ago. Her breasts used to turn heads but after nursing two kids they're like two sacks of pudding and the enlarged nipples have become overly sensitive. His stroking burns slightly and she has to grit her teeth. The feeling passes and is now okay, then more than okay. Wren sighs loudly once, twice, the signal for him to move on. He reaches between her legs. She reaches between his. They fondle each other in familiar ways until Wren initiates the taking off of her pajama bottoms – the "all ready" sign. Greg removes his boxers.

He lifts her knee, just so. After fitting himself in, he reaches back around to continue to do his part but Wren's hand is already there.

"Let me," she says shyly.

Greg stops, suddenly wider awake. "Have I been doing something wrong?" His sour breath blasts her face.

"No, not at all."

"Here," he says, slipping his hand under hers. "Show me what you want." He kisses the back of her neck.

"It's okay," she mumbles and removes her hand.

She thinks she might not get there today, but habit has its way and soon her pleasure begins its heady climb. She comes with a breathy moan: one good one. Then Greg removes his hand to hold her hips with two hands, his orgasm punctuated by three frozen seconds followed by a great rush of unwashed breath. They snuggle after, her head over his heart, which thuds dangerously fast, or so it seems. She imagines a heart attack, 911 panic, mouth-to-mouth, the shock and thump of chest paddles. What if?

"Eggs Florentine or waffles?" says Greg, one foot stabbing for his boxers, lost somewhere under the covers.

"Either's fine with me, sweetheart." She reaches for her glasses.

"AND HOW ARE YOU TODAY?" Wren refers to her sheet. "Mr. Haspray? Or do you prefer Timothy or Tim?" Or ponytail guy, she says to herself, thinking how ultraclean his honey-coloured hair is, how flyaway soft, like a child's. She sees his birthdate. He's twenty-seven and very tan, as if he's just returned from some exotic location. The shadow of a beard darkens his strong jawline and emphasizes the circles under his eyes. Her daughter has those. Allergic shiners, the doctor calls them.

"Call me Lex."

Lex? His eyes, an unusually bright blue, are staring at her now, like her kids do when they're wanting something from her. She looks away. "Uh, okay, Lex. So you've had your water?"

"Yes, all of it."

"Let's just see here if your bladder's full. If you can lower your trousers a bit for me."

He flicks open the hidden buttons of his fly with a deft hand. Here we go, she thinks, taking sheets of paper toweling and tucking it around the lowered waist of his jeans. His stomach is tanned and muscled. She doesn't see a tan line or any sign of underwear. Squeezing the warmed tube of gel, she squirts a blob onto his abdomen. The tube makes a long gassy sound.

"Have to refill that one," she says, colour rushing to her cheeks.

"Hey, no problem." His voice is suddenly an octave deeper. "And your name is?"

She hesitates. What's with the voice? "Wren."

"Wren," he repeats in his new baritone. "Sweet bird."

Please, she thinks, and reaches behind to dim the lights. Adjusting her glasses, she steadies her eyes on the screen while gliding the transducer over his bladder. She feels him staring again.

"Bladder's nice and full. We can go ahead with the sonogram," she confirms.

"Any fuller and it would burst," he says with a manly chuckle.

Wren just smiles. In the dimmed light, he's moviestar handsome without the personality, the suavity. "Sure is getting dark early these days," she says, correcting the brightness of the screen.

He doesn't respond so she glances over. He's staring intently at her chest, breathing through parted lips.

Oh, grow up, she thinks, and perversely straightens up, puffing out her chest.

He crosses his arms and shuts his eyes and she feels she's won some small victory.

She slides the instrument back and forth. Bowels perfectly normal, she can tell already, and decides to cut this short, stop wasting his time and hers. She lifts the transducer and his eyes pop open.

"The pain's lower down," he says, his baritone softly desperate.

She sighs, replaces the transducer a touch lower. Was this worth a free lunch?

He slides up on the bed in one quick jerk, causing her hand to dip down in his pubic hair. She pulls the instrument away, then sees the very substantial bulge in his pants.

"There, all done. You can clean yourself up now." Her throat has narrowed and her voice cracks. Act normal and leave the room, she tells herself, switching on the light.

He groans at the sudden brightness.

"Aren't you supposed to do my kidneys?" he says.

Don't look at him, she tells herself. "That's been done recently enough. It's not necessary." She's talking too fast.

"But I thought it was...procedure."

"Maybe next time," she says, gaining control. "I have another patient. The bathroom is two doors down to your right."

She gathers her clipboard and leaves, closing the door behind her. She waits in the staff room, more awake than she's felt all day, listening for his exit. Finally hearing the creak of the door, she peeks around the corner. Ponytail guy is staring back at her, a small, grateful-looking smile on his face. Wren pulls her head back, her heart racing.

She returns to her room to ready it for the next patient and there's a wad of paper towelling balled up on her chair. Ew. The paper's placement is obviously deliberate. Maybe he's got a thing for women in lab coats. But why me and not Shannon? Donning latex gloves, she pinches up the towelling and throws it in the garbage.

"THE WEEKEND," sighs Shannon as she and Wren cross the parking lot, car keys jangling in her hand like an alarm. "Ryan's taking me to Café Mozart. Ever been?"

"Never even heard of it."

"Oh god, it's the best place. They serve like twenty types of martinis and this amazing osso busco dish."

Osso what?

"They play great music, despite their name. Maybe get Greg to take you for your birthday."

"That's an idea," says Wren over the roof of her brown Wagovan. Her fortieth, tomorrow. God, she hopes he hasn't planned anything for tonight. She didn't even wash her hair this morning and just wants to flake out on the couch with a movie. Maybe the new James Bond if it's out.

"I bought a new teddy at La Boutique," says Shannon, "navy silk with slits in all the right places."

"Have fun," Wren says, opening her door. How many slits could there be?

"You too," she hears before pulling the door shut.

Shannon gets into her white Volkswagen beetle, the new "space bug" as Greg calls it, a white silk rose in the vase attached to the dash. She wonders if that vase is plastic or glass. Shannon wiggles her manicured nails goodbye and she and her fake rose purr away.

Wren flips down the visor and checks her face in the mirror. What if she got contacts? She ruffles her hair. How about bangs? Would Greg be inspired to make love on a Monday? She laughs out loud.

"That's mean," she says aloud and, smiling, starts up the car. A red light brightens the dash. Should fill up now. James has a basketball tournament in Nanaimo early tomorrow. "So much for sleeping in." She punches on the radio. CBC. A radio drama's playing, about a shooting of a doctor who performs abortions. She turns it off. The day's been depressing enough. Sadly, Wren recalls her four o'clock. Cheerful, polite, not much older than Shannon. She was in a hurry to get home to her ten-month-old, her girl.

"Finally had my girl after two boys," she'd said. When she smiled, her cheeks had long dimples in them. "My husband cried he was so happy."

The ovarian tumours looked like hunchbacked spiders, or ticks with their heads burrowed under the skin. Perfectly round and well-established, they were in for the long haul. Wren knew this young woman (Laurie?) was a terminal, two years at best. And most of that time would be ruined by fear and hospitals, estrangement from her kids and from herself. You didn't feel quite as sick when the person was past their prime. But god, the woman was breastfeeding.

A good portion of her ultrasound training was devoted to not reacting to what came up on the screen. They practiced poker faces while asking the names of children, discussing weather, the advantages and disadvantages of pets. Wren sometimes felt like a seer, reading a patient's future in the cups of their organs. Some patients are desperate to know what she knows, have lost a week's sleep already, can't bear to wait a minute longer. Some plead, muster tears; twice she's been offered money.

"You'll have to wait to hear from your doctor," she says ten times a day. "I'd be out of a job if I took over his. Or hers," she's always quick to add. She says this with a smile in her voice, a pat on the shoulder or knee. This woman today just said thanks afterwards and squeezed Wren's hand.

The gas station looks inviting, all lit up in the draining light. Wren pulls in to the full-serve side. She's put in her week, doesn't mind paying extra to have someone wait on her.

"Fill her up?" says the young attendant. "Check the oil?"

"Uh..." Wren digs into her wallet for her Esso card. "Twenty's worth, please."

"Oil check?" he repeats.

"Sure, go ahead. It's been awhile." She unlatches the hood, pops the gas cover.

After hooking up the gas pump, the kid skips around to the front of the car. Wren watches him bunch his lips as he struggles to open the hood. He has full shapely lips. Every man under thirty is good-looking to her these days. Elastic skin, shiny hair, this kid's not yet twenty-five.

"He's beautiful," she whispers before he disappears behind the raised hood.

He checks the oil, then runs to catch the gas pump from overriding the twenty mark. He could probably make love all night long and again after breakfast. She snickers. He lets the hood down gently and comes around to the window. His face is suddenly serious.

"You'll need to come inside," he says with new authority, "to pay."

"Here, just take my card?"

"Oh, well, no," he stutters, "there's been a lot of fraudulent claims lately. I need to check your signature."

The words ring static, meaningless, and the kid is signalling her with his head now.

"I need you inside," his voice is almost urgent.

Maybe he likes older women, she jokes to herself. Guys this age can be horny all the time. His eyes dart nervously up and down the car.

"Sorry for the inconvenience." He's not budging.

"Fine. I'll just move the car," she sighs.

"No, leave it."

"But what if –."

"We won't be long."

Can't wait another second to get her inside? She undoes her seat belt, groans as her stiff knees straighten to stand. Following him into the station, she's startled at how small his bum looks from behind. A child's bottom. Hardly enticing. She stifles a laugh.

Inside, he hurries behind the counter and grabs the phone.

"There's a guy on the floor of your back seat," he says breathless and staring past her outside. "I'll call the police."

"There's a guy in my car?" She doesn't understand.

"Yeah, on the floor in the back."

The room's fluorescent lights are suddenly cartoon bright. "But why is he..." Wren's voice fades. She's afraid to turn around and look.

An older man in grease-stained overalls and stinking of nicotine comes in from the garage.

"Sam, there's a man on the floor in the back of this woman's car," the boy tells the mechanic.

"No kiddin?"

"I'm calling the – yeah, I'm calling from the Esso at Shellbourne and McKenzie?"

"Hey, here he goes," says Sam and they all turn to watch. Wren too.

The far door is open and a figure springs up and starts running. A honey-coloured ponytail flaps up and down on the back of his navy blue sweatshirt.

"A girl?" asks the older man squinting.

"No, a guy," mumbles Wren.

"Old boyfriend of yours?" The mechanic wears a cockeyed smile.

The kid's finished on the phone and comes around the counter. He puts his hand gently on Wren's shoulder.

"Jesus, that's crazy," he says, shaking his head. "You okay?"

"Yeah, thanks," she says weakly. Her heart thrums with adrenalin. She just now realizes what this kid's done. "Thank you so much," she tries again with more enthusiasm.

"Sure, no problem. Hey, if you know the guy you can have him charged."

Wren can't think to answer. Another car has pulled up to the full-service pump and he moves towards the door. "Want me to move your car? The police should be here any minute."

"Yes, okay. Thanks again for what you've done."

He smiles his full-lipped smile and she notices, for the first time, how one of his eyes swings unattractively to the right.

SHE DRIVES THE REST OF THE WAY HOME with both hands on the wheel and her daughter's favourite pop music station on the radio. She doesn't understand the lyrics, something about lonely gods, but the melody is soothing.

The house is dark as she pulls into the driveway. Greg's bike is here. Friday. He'll be on the back deck having a beer. As she locks the car door, she studies the dark floor of the back seat. He was lying there, close enough to reach up between the seats and touch her. She hurries up the front steps, a tight grip on her keys. We really need to fix the porch light, she thinks, scanning the dark beyond. She fumbles the key in the lock. It seems to take forever to open. She slips inside, pulling the door shut behind her with a defining click. It's black in the hall and living room. Not one light on. Isn't Greg home yet? And the kids? Could *he* know where she lives? Her chest tightens. It's hard to breathe.

"Greg," she whimpers into the dark.

"Surprise," comes one thunderous voice as light illuminates twenty, thirty, forty savagely grinning faces, Shannon's included.

Wren hides her face in her hands and tears start from her eyes. People are laughing and yelling "Happy Birthday." Now Greg's sweatered arm is around her and she buries her face in its warmth, the familiar musk of his deodorant. Her hands grope his bare neck and for a split second she imagines a pony-tail where there's none.

"Surprised?" says Greg laughing into her ear.

Yes and no, she thinks, unable to speak.

Best Friends

THE MEMBERS-ONLY CLUB WAS PACKED. Vancouver was tied in the playoffs 3–3, and tonight's outcome would either send the Canucks into the third round or onto the golf course. Grayson Dawe, Kelly's husband, had got an assist for what had been the only goal scored that night until the Colorado Avalanche tied it up in the game's last twenty seconds. Now the game would be decided in sudden-death overtime. The volume on the giant flat screen magically quieted and the thrum of conversation took over.

"I hate overtime," groaned Cindi.

"God, me too," said Kelly. Her left leg vibrated under the table. She couldn't make it stop. This was Grayson's first time in the playoffs and she knew how much a win tonight would mean to him. She looked towards the entrance. Where the hell was Joan, anyway? It hadn't been easy wrangling that guest pass.

"But even if we lose," Cindi squeezed Kelly's arm, "Grayson's the reason the team's made it this far."

Kelly pictured Grayson's postgoal face, his eyes blasted open with pure happiness. He once confessed to her that the greatest moments in his life were on the ice just after scoring. "It's such a rush," he told her. "But it's not an ego thing, just the opposite. It's like the barriers are gone between me and the other players and we're just one burst of...well, joy. I mean, it's just as great if Marek scores, Daniel, or a rookie even."

Grayson could talk to her like that. And she could confide in him too. By now, she considered him her best friend and couldn't help feeling a little jealous of those feelings he shared with his fellow players. The only thing in her own experience she thought might be the equivalent were the rare times – she could count them on one hand, minus three fingers – that she and Gray achieved simultaneous orgasms. When she couldn't separate her pleasure from his and felt almost painfully close to him afterwards.

"You can't discount Marek's defensive play," she said, and drained the dregs of her wine. "Really, Grayson's playing so much better since Marek came on board. They're so attuned to each other out there. I'd venture to say Marek's the reason we're in the playoffs at all."

"Well, it is so nice for them to be on the same team again. And I don't miss Boston one bit. Too damn cold in the winter and the summers are boiling."

Marek had been best man at her and Grayson's wedding last spring and Grayson was best man at

Cindi and Marek's the year before. The guys had known each other for years: they met playing junior and then played together on Vancouver's farm team in Manitoba. But then Marek was drafted by Boston. He'd been trying to get traded to Vancouver ever since and, finally, with Grayson's help, it happened. Kelly and Cindi had only recently started getting together on their own and Kelly was still conscious of making a good impression. She crossed her spastic knee over her other leg and her freed foot tapped at the air.

"Love your boots," said Cindi.

"Thanks." Kelly'd never spent so much money on a pair of shoes.

"I almost bought the very same ones in blue. There's nothing like Italian leather." She scanned the room and signalled their waiter. "I need another drink."

"I could use one, too," said a voice behind Kelly.

"Joan." She stood and hugged her oldest friend. "You made it."

"Didn't think the manimal at the door was going to let me in."

"Scottie only looks dangerous," said Cindi. "He's a prince in disguise."

"Joan, this is Cindi, Marek's wife. Cindi, this is Joan. Joan and I have been best friends since grade nine."

"Eight," corrected Joan.

Kelly watched them shake hands. Cindi in her spiked heeled boots, snug jeans and push-up bra, Joan in dirty hiking boots, the baggy green army pants

Kelly used to covet and a black suit jacket with a cluster of political symbols pinned to the lapel.

"Now *those* look dangerous," said Joan pointing to Cindi's nails. Kelly knew what Joan thought of acrylic nails, of any kind of nails, and the money spent on them. Kelly was considering getting hers done, mostly to help her stop biting them. The only reason she didn't was Joan.

"They are," said Cindi.

"Sorry I'm so late," said Joan. "I had gross amounts of marking to do. Then I missed the damn bus."

Kelly had offered to pay for a cab, but Joan, too environmentally correct for cabs, had refused. "Joan's doing her masters in English. She's a TA," Kelly explained to Cindi.

"Do you want to be a teacher?" asked Cindi as their waiter arrived. "I'll have the Vantini this time, Vance. For luck. Do you guys want one?"

"Vantini?" said Joan, blinking.

"It's a blue Curacao martini with Bombay Sapphire gin and three black olives on a red stick," explained the waiter.

"Sounds fancy," said Joan. This was her euphemism for expensive. "I'll have whatever she's having." She pointed at Kelly.

"Sure, two more Vantini's. For luck."

"You getting as superstitious as Grayson?" said Joan.

"On your tab, Mrs. Dawe?"

"Please."

"You don't have to pay for mine, Mrs. Dawe," said Joan.

"I know," said Kelly. "But you're my guest. So shut up."

Marrying Grayson had included marrying money. A couple million a year. Kelly went from sharing a one-bedroom basement dungeon in the burbs with Joan to a three-bedroom downtown penthouse. From taking public transit to driving a nifty little hybrid. Money was one more thing that came between them now.

"To answer your question," Joan said to Cindi, "I hope to be a scholar. My thesis is on the evolution of the female novelist. Can you...do you read?"

Behave yourself, thought Kelly, suppressing a smile.

"I like the Irish writer, Marian Keyes," said Cindi. "She's hilarious. Even when she's talking about cancer or divorce she can make you laugh."

Joan pinched at her nose and caught Kelly's eye. This was their old signal that something was beneath them. Having always been hard on herself, Joan felt perfectly justified in being hard on others.

"Oh yeah, I've heard she's a great read," lied Kelly. She glanced at Joan.

"I've got all her books, if you ever want to borrow any. Great vacation reading."

"Thanks."

"I've got a new one for you, Kel." Joan kept Kelly "educated" about the latest novels. "By Booker winner, Kiran Desai. I'll bring it to lunch this week."

"Great. Two new authors," said Kelly.

The drinks were delivered along with another complimentary bowl of curried cashews.

"To moving on to the next round," toasted Cindi.

"To Planet Hockey," added Joan.

"You're incorrigible," muttered Kelly, pinching Joan's thigh under the table.

"Ouch." Joan grabbed up her hand, smiled and kissed it.

Planet Hockey was another of Joan's euphemisms. This one for male stupidity. When Kelly started getting serious about Grayson, Joan had been incredulous. "A hockey player? Don't be distracted by his pecs, Kel," – Kelly had a thing for nice pecs – "pecs will grow flaccid and then you'll be all alone."

"His is a different kind of intelligence," she had defended. "It's more...intuitive and sensual."

"It's called the animal realm," Joan had scoffed.

"He takes me out of my head, Joan, makes me inhabit my skin. Maybe it is simple-minded but... well, life just *feels* more satisfying."

That had shut her up and Joan had stopped putting Grayson down after that. Now she only needled Kelly about not going for a second degree, about "short-changing herself for money." Kelly forgave her friend, though. Joan didn't made friends easily and her relationships with men seemed to have a three-month expiry. As a result, she was possessive of Kelly's friendship.

The players were returning to the ice, the volume on the TV filling the room again. Kelly's jiggling leg had calmed down but now it started up again.

"What number's Grayson?" asked Joan. "I forget."

"Sixteen."

"The merit of sports, Joan," said Kelly, "if, that is, you can open your mind for one minute, is that it's totally unplanned and spontaneous. Just like good literature, hockey creates expectations."

Joan didn't have a comeback, which meant she was impressed. One point for me, thought Kelly. "And hockey's sexy," she added. "And sexy wakes you up."

"Sexy," said Joan, "is a very subjective experience."

The whistle blew. Overtime had begun.

Daniel won the faceoff and passed it to Marek who instantly found the centre of Grayson's stick.

"Ooh, they're in sync," said Cindi over the rising cheers.

"Kelly tells me that Marek wears a laminated picture of his mother inside his game skate, under his heel," said Joan.

Cindi laughed. "His right heel. Just one of those things." She shook her head. "What can I say?"

"How does he feel about his mother, stepping on her face that way?"

"It's complicated," said Cindi. "She disowned him."

"Why?"

Kelly nudged Joan for being so nosy.

"They just didn't get along, I guess. I was hoping she'd come to the wedding but no go."

"No come," corrected Joan.

A groan went up from the bar as a Vancouver shot went off the post.

"They all have their luck rituals," said Cindi.

"Gray does some weird shoe thing, doesn't he?" Joan asked Kelly.

"Yeah."

"What does he do again?" asked Cindi. "Something with the order he —"

"Well, he has an order that he puts his gear on, starting with his cup and ending with his mouthguard. And he reverses all that when he takes things off."

"So complicated," sighed Cindi.

"It's habit for him now, but occasionally he'll space out and put, like, his mouthguard in before his helmet and then, believe it or not, he'll take all his gear off and start over, right from his cup."

"Psy-cho," sang Joan.

Kelly laughed. "And, yes, it's always his left sock and skate first before his right, which goes for his socks and shoes too."

Joan shook her head.

"See number twenty, there? Orlovski?" said Cindi pointing. "He has to tap his stick on the boards three times before each of his shifts and pat every player on the back three times before each period. It drives the guys crazy."

Colorado intercepted the puck for a breakaway and Cindi grabbed Kelly's hand. Kelly's jiggling leg froze and out of the corner of her eye she saw Joan take note of their entwined hands before turning her attention to the screen. The room rumbled with worry as the Avalanche winger, all cocky speed and open ice, bore down on the Canuck goalie.

"No fuckin' way," shouted a guy at the bar.

The Avalanche player took his best shot and the goalie's right hand flew skyward, his legs springing open like a runner jumping a hurdle. For seconds after, no one, not even the goalie himself, was sure where the puck had gone. Then he opened his glove and the puck dropped to the ice.

The bar erupted in nervous guffaws and high fives. Cindi released Kelly's hand, and shook her fists in the air. "We love you, Bobby Lou."

Heart kicking at her ribs, Kelly let out a moan and rubbed her finger where Cindi's nail had dug in.

"It's supposed to be a game, not torture," said Joan.

Kelly sipped her drink. "I just know how much Grayson wants this."

Joan nodded her understanding. "Come on, you Canukleheads," she cheered loudly, making Kelly laugh.

The next faceoff gave Vancouver the puck and when Vladmir snuck it through the legs of his check, the pumped-up bar started shouting.

"Yes! Go! Shoot!"

Vladmir shouldered a guy into the boards, then crossed the puck to Marek on the far side of the net. Without even a backwards glance, Marek hooked the puck behind him to Grayson's stick. This sightless move threw off Grayson's check, and Grayson, now centred in front of the net, lifted the puck with a delicate flick of his wrist into the top right corner.

The room roared to its feet bringing Kelly with it. For a moment, she felt like she was best friends with every person here. People spontaneously hugged their neighbours and someone was patting her back, saying "good man you got there." She smiled, nodding stupidly.

A voice rose about the cheering. "Hey! What was that?"

All eyes turned to the screen where, in slow motion, the oversized TV began to replay the winning goal, then Grayson's defenseless eyes and bursting smile, a smile Kelly felt glowing in the pit of her stomach. Then her husband's mouth ever so slowly puckered up as he cinched Marek's neck in his elbow, and kissed him lips to lips, his eyes drifting closed.

A collective "Ugh" rose from the crowd like a bad smell.

"What the hell?" said someone at the table in front of them.

"Dawe's not even Russian," said another.

"Or French."

The bartender called out that the next drink was on the house and the room erupted anew.

"What is this, a roomful of homophobes?" said Joan.

Kelly looked from Joan to Cindi who was staring at the TV, her lips pressed together.

"Don't see that kind of thanks very often," offered one sports commentator.

"Not on the lips," answered the other, his voice a grimace.

"Heroes are so quickly demonized. Just ask Atwood," said Joan, but Kelly wasn't listening. She had seen how quickly Marek had pushed his way under the clutch of celebrating players to go knock helmets with the goalie. And now she recognized the hurt in Grayson's eyes before he donned a tough half-smile and punched his gloved hand into the gloves of his other teammates. Cindi excused herself to the washroom.

LICKING HER FOREFINGER, Kelly tested the iron. Hot. She looked out the bank of windows in the living room and breathed in the view of the North Shore mountains looming above the harbour. To welcome home Grayson, due any minute now, she'd filled the CD tray with his favourites. Our Lady Peace filtered out of the sound system and into every room in the apartment. She removed her new shirt from its shopping bag. It was a tailored shirt by Jacob, form fitting, in Grayson's favourite red, and she wanted to wear it for him. She hooked the shirt collar over the neck of the ironing board and recalled last night's *Coaches' Corner,* which Don Cherry had renamed Kissing Corner.

"Not only is Dawe a great stickhandler, the guy can kiss too," Cherry had joked.

His straight man had tears in his eyes from laughing.

"Well, these guys can get pretty close," quipped Cherry. "Like girlfriends."

This morning's *Vancouver Sun,* delivered with a thud against her front door, had a picture of Grayson's closed-eyed kiss in vivid colour. The headline, "The

Kiss That Tells All," made Kelly furious for its obscure double meaning.

Grayson's mother had called first thing that morning to ask if Kelly'd heard from Gray, if he was all right. They both knew how Grayson hated being made a big deal of, even when it was pure praise.

"No, but I'm sure he's fine," said Kelly, not wanting to encourage her mother-in-law's talent for fretting. Usually it concerned the roughness of the game, "those terrible checks from behind that put boys in wheelchairs for life." Or about Grayson losing his "perfect teeth. Other mothers envied me his straight teeth." Or the athlete's plight of early knee and hip replacements. This morning she'd talked about the "ill-intentioned media" and "Grayson's sensitive, caring nature." Kelly wanted to hang up before she shared something creepy, like a boyhood fascination with women's shoes.

She'd been fielding calls all day. Mostly media wanting to know how she felt about last night's kiss. Not how she felt about him winning the round for his team and the fans, but about that damn kiss. She had finally turned off the phone, checking her messages periodically to see if Cindi called. Cindi had left right after the game, said she had an early Pilates class the next day. Kelly finished ironing the shirt and put it on. She could have called Cindi but didn't. She wasn't sure why. Checking herself in the mirrored wall of the dining room, she undid the shirt's top button.

The apartment buzzer went and Kelly turned off the iron.

"Hello," she said into the intercom.

"Hey, Kel. It's Joan. Let me in."

Kelly buzzed her up, then thought of how she could keep it short so Joan wasn't here when Grayson got home. Joan probably thought, as usual, that she needed saving, but she didn't.

"I tried to call but couldn't get through," said Joan. "You all right?

"I'm fine," Kelly sighed.

"What a lot of bullshit people are making of that kiss."

"Yeah, I know."

"That's a nice shirt. New?"

"Yes, it's new, Joan. Sorry." Joan wore only *recycled* clothes. The two of them used to hit up all the second-hand places together.

"As long as it's not made in China."

"No, it's not made in China," she said, though she hadn't a clue where it was made.

"Did you know cotton is the most heavily pesticided crop in the world?"

"Didn't know." She went ahead into the kitchen. "Coffee?"

"Do I ever say no?" Joan drank coffee like it was water. "God, I'll never get over this fucking view."

Hitting the mountains dead-on, the sun had turned them a shimmery purple and the harbour below looked like melted silver.

Kelly pressed the warming button on the coffee maker and Joan settled herself on a stool at the counter. "Mmm, do I smell your lasagna?"

"Yep."

"Caesar salad and French loaf from Parisian Bakery? Italian red?"

"Caesar and foccacia from Tony's. Beer. Grayson's not a big wine drinker."

"Too bad."

"Joan, Grayson will be home soon. I'd invite you to stay for dinner but it's not a good night."

"I understand," said Joan. "Knowing your sensitive man, he'll be pretty upset. And even if they are gay, it shouldn't —"

"You're talking about my husband, Joan. Remember?"

"Well, bisexual."

"Joan. I'm not listening."

"Well, I think it's inevitable in any all-boys school —"

"You'd love nothing better than to see my marriage fail, wouldn't you? Sex aside, Grayson and I are best friends, Joan." She knew calling Grayson her best friend would hurt a little but Joan deserved it. She heard Gray's key in the lock. "He's home," she whispered. "Just don't say anything...for my sake."

The front door creaked opened

"Hey Grayson," she called out in an upbeat voice. "I'm in the kitchen with Joan."

"Hey girls."

"Welcome home," called Joan.

Kelly pictured him sitting down on the hall bench, taking off his right shoe first, then his left. She met him in the kitchen doorway, cupped his playoff beard between her hands and kissed him hello. His moustache pricked the skin under her nose.

"Congratulations on your win last night," called Joan, and Grayson pulled his mouth from Kelly's.

"Yeah, thanks." He smiled weakly on one side of his face in that cool-boy way of his that Kelly always found sexy. He looked tired. "How are you, Joan?"

"Bogged down with marking, on top of my thesis. But I made my own bed, so can't complain."

"How did *this* happen?" asked Kelly. Grayson had a sizable cut under his eyebrow. She made him tip his head downwards and saw how the accompanying bruise shaded his eyelid purple, a burnt edge of yellow.

"Ah, stick in the face. It's nothing," Grayson said, sidestepping her to the fridge. He was invariably dismissive about the beatings his body took. He took out a beer, spun off the top, pulled on it long and hard.

"You must fly over the Rockies between Denver and here," said Joan.

Grayson nodded. Kelly wished Joan wasn't here.

"Is it beautiful?"

"It was today. The sun was out and it turned the snow a pale blue."

"Nice."

There was a pause as if he'd rather not ask while Joan was there but just couldn't wait. "You get any calls, Kel?" He thumbed through the pile of mail that had collected since he'd left five days ago.

"Well," she didn't want to tell him so soon. "Your mother called...and the Associated Press and TSN."

"What did you tell TSN?" Grayson pulled on the bottle again, held a letter up to the light. Joan sat quietly watching. Like a big fat fly on the wall, thought Kelly.

"Oh, god, I don't know. Said you were excited is all. You've taken them to the third round, Grayson. You should have heard the screaming in the bar."

Grayson smirked, a hiccup of pride.

"It was insane," chimed in Joan. "There were even Vantinis on the house."

"Nice." He caught Kelly's eye. "What else did you say, Kel?"

"I told her that you and Marek met as juniors at UBC." She took a breath. "She wanted to know if you roomed together on the road. I told her that you're happily married in every sense of the word, thank you very much."

Grayson shook his head and stared out the window. The sun was now setting, the sky all purples and pinks.

"It'll blow over," she said, taking down a mug and hesitating before pouring Joan's coffee. It wasn't quite hot, but maybe she'd get the hint. "The guys giving you a hard time?"

"Kelly, just say no comment next time, okay?" He downed the remains of the bottle and left the kitchen. He never spoke to her like that. Joan reached for Kelly's hand but she pulled away.

"Sorry, Joan, but we really need to be alone right now."

"Sure," said Joan, standing. She took a long sip of coffee. "I'm here for you, Kelly. You know that, right?"

As soon as Joan left, Grayson took another beer from the fridge and sat down at the computer in the breakfast nook. Kelly grabbed a beer for herself, took a healthy swig and went to stand behind him. Afraid to say anything, she just ran her nails over his scalp the way he liked, and looked over his shoulder at the screen. *Forward Dawe, The Ottawa Citizen*, she read just before it clicked away.

Le Soleil's sports page came up next. *"Baisee de Mort."*

Mort is death, Kelly recalled from high school French, but what is *baisee*?

The screen cut back to the desktop pictures Kelly had put together for him. Bobby Hull, Guy Lafleur, Gretzky, Lemieux and other Hall of Famers.

"I can't believe I did that," he said softly.

"You'd won the game," she said.

Grayson was silent and Kelly didn't know what to do except keep stroking his head.

"He wouldn't talk to me," he said finally, his voice a whisper.

"Marek," she coughed out, the name a fishbone in her throat.

Grayson swivelled around in his chair and took hold of Kelly's waist. His large hands with the fastidiously clean nails, a habit she loved about him, pulled her between his knees. He laid his head on her chest. Kelly looked down at her husband, her best friend, and kept stroking. His eyes closed and she was afraid he might cry. She'd never seen him cry, not even when his wrist was broken at an exhibition game and one splintered end poked up through the skin. She studied the tiny sunset of a bruise on his eyelid and pressed his head closer.

She flashed on his handsome face filling the screen and the slow-motion kiss he'd given his best man. His eye wasn't cut then, she realized.

"I'm here for you, Grayson," she said and kissed the top of his head.

He nodded, his beard making small rasping sounds against her new shirt.

What's Handed Down

THEY WERE MY SISTER'S OLD SHOES. Mom had threaded them with brand new laces, looped them in smart bows. I could smell the polish where she'd touched up the scuff marks.

"They're stupid and I won't wear them," I said, furious at the shoes for fitting. Already broken in, they were comfortable too.

"Yes, you will," Mom shot back in a tone that surprised me.

She was easygoing as moms went, especially with me, her distant third and rather self-sufficient child. Perhaps my willfulness surprised her too, but since turning ten I had become savvy to what was cool and what was not. Loafers with tassels were cool; saddle shoes were not. Wearing these to school on Monday would be fatal.

"I won't," I said and held my mother's eye.

There were tiny ruts etched around her eyes and one big rut slicing her forehead in half. Her skin looked worn, looked handed down. Her mouth sagged open for three weary seconds before the whole package snapped awake.

"You will wear these shoes," she said, squeezing what I knew was a big voice into a small one, "until you wear them out."

She strode down the hall to her bedroom, closed the door hard behind her. I was unmoved. Last Saturday, Mom had bought my sister new shoes. Loafers with tassels. It wasn't fair. Not by a mile.

I LIE IN MY BEDROOM while, out in the living room, my four-year-old eats no-name cereal in front of insipidly violent cartoons. This morning my husband was the one who made breakfast and lunches simultaneously, signed crumpled permission slips, hunted down matching socks, brushed knotted screaming hair and resistant teeth, cursed zippers before dropping the two boys at school. This made him late for work, but I didn't care. Couldn't care. I open my eyes enough to make out the red digits shining from the bedside clock. Nine forty and I still can't move. I imagine a headache if I do get up. How is it that some days lose all meaning and life becomes effort? I imagine the freedom to stay in bed all day, slipping in and out of sleep, waking at times to read or daydream. I imagine being served sliced fruit and a hot drink by some kind, foreign-tongued maid. What I can't imagine is getting up, getting dressed and petting the whimpering dog, which lies in wait amongst a minefield of Lego outside my bedroom door. Unloading the dishwasher, filling it again, washing the gummy oatmeal pot, digging out the food scum from the drain basket, cleaning the counter of crumbs, crumbs, crumbs, sweeping, sweeping, sweeping the floor, doing another load of laundry while keeping my youngest wholesomely occupied until it's time to feed her again and do more dishes, drain scum, crumbs and floor, find a bag without holes and walk the dog, then push her on the backyard swing while singing a song of six pence, over and over, as if it were a round.

It's the repetition that defeats me. How breakfast becomes lunch becomes dinner becomes breakfast... How a bed takes ten minutes to make and one second to ruin, ten minutes to make, one second to ruin... How fingernails refuse to stay cut... How dust and dog hair conspire to mock you...

I remember being a kid in school, bored behind a desk, sitting, sitting, and sitting some more (because standing had consequences), and dreaming of the day when I'd be an adult free to do what I wanted, when I wanted. Today, I want the world to go –

"Mommy?" My daughter's expectant call weights my stomach with responsibility. This feeling lasts three, maybe five, seconds before I surrender to indifference.

"Mommy?" Louder this time.

Little slippered feet come shushing down the hall and I curl onto my side, tuck my head in. I am a giant wood-bug. My four-year-old fumbles noisily with the doorknob before the door creaks open.

"Are you still asleep?" she asks in her cute but needy voice.

My eyes are carefully closed. I don't answer. Earlier I'd said Mommy was sick and had to rest. It's what my mother used to say from the large bed in her darkened room, the drapes blotting out the day, the heavy bedspread pulled up to her ears. I wonder, now, whether or not she was really sick or, like me, just needing to escape.

"I finished my cereal," my daughter says into the quiet. She pauses, all ears, then tries again, "I'm thirsty."

I don't answer and the door is softly pulled closed, slippers shushing back down the hall, fading to nothing.

I RETIED THE LACES in double knots, then got my new pink and white Schwinn from the patio. I'd received the bike for my tenth birthday six weeks ago. Unlike the shoes, it was exactly what I'd asked for.

Our low-rise apartment complex was built on a slope, the buildings arranged like two horseshoes, one inside the other. Separating them was a wide U-shaped street with parking spaces on either side. I biked to the top of our side of the horseshoe and started down. I let the force of gravity do its thing, took my feet off the pedals and planted the tips of my sister's shoes on the rugged asphalt. The shoes made a satisfying scraping sound as they dragged along below me, vibrations ringing my ankles. I pictured the leather blistering apart, hoping this might speed the process along. When I reached the bottom of the hill, I pedalled furiously up to the top of the other side, turned around and did it again.

MY BED LIES ALONGSIDE glass doors to a small moss-riddled deck. These doors have blinds to block the morning sun, but I never use them because I love falling asleep viewing the night sky. I find solace in its platter of stars, or in watching the soundless beep of a plane's red light as it moves across the sky at what seems like blimp speed. These days the planet Mars outshines the stars with its closeness, its stolen fire. I find the existence of other planets, however uninhabitable, to be cheering. And sometimes there's the sudden blaze of a shooting star, which registers a second after the seeing and leaves me wishing for something I don't understand.

Framing my window of sky is what I consider the weeping willow of fir trees, a Deodara Cedar. Its muscular trunk curves suggestively and its fanned branches, like giant's hands, sweep the air with the softest of spankings. This morning, despite the cold drizzle, despite the toxic fumes from a truck idling across the street, she remains tall and quiescent, content to do what trees must do. Day after day.

"How do you manage it?" I mumble against my pillow.

Invisible wind lifts the branch closest to me and sets it back down with a stroke like love itself. I close my eyes.

IT WAS GAINING ON DINNERTIME. People arriving home from work forced me and my bike to the side of the street. I thought of my father in his furniture shop downtown. The Tropic Shop. Rattan. I liked saying the word rattan. Like a gun shot into wind that word. Daddy was closing up shop later these days, and wouldn't be home for another couple hours yet. His dinner would be kept in the oven, hidden under tinfoil.

My thighs were aching, my feet numb, my self-righteousness nearly spent. I pulled over to examine the damage. The plastic caps on the ends of the new laces were black and split, the shoes' bulbous tips frayed into a close-cut gray leather beard. There was one spot on the left shoe where a kind of stiff netting showed through and, behind that, my navy sock.

I felt a mean-eyed sense of power. I'd done it. I'd worn the shoes out, just like she said. Normally I was an obedient child, a people pleaser, so this feeling was foreign to me. Foreign and therefore exciting. I felt proud of myself and my shoes, and imagined tucking them away at the back of my closet like a tarnished trophy. I parked my bike back on the patio, caught my slim smile in the window.

Inside, I was met by the smell of potato onion soup. I hated potato onion soup. I heard the television.

talking in my brother's room, then the whirr of my mother's sewing machine. She had a sewing corner set up in the walk-in dressing room off her bedroom. I didn't hesitate, didn't even knock on her closed bedroom door. One shoe hanging on finger hooks from each hand, the undone laces dangling hopelessly, I strode into her sanctuary.

I'M DREAMING OF SOMETHING that actually happened to me. I was maybe seven. A crowded beach, loud with surf, complaining gulls, splashing humans. The waves are dangerously big, and I am hanging onto a raft with my mother. We must paddle our feet at heart speed towards the rising wall of water to safely make it over top. This wave breaks sooner than later and the raft flips. I am snatched in a watery fist and dragged under, somersaulted, my head scrubbing the sand. I come up for air just as another wave slaps me back under. Where is the raft? Where is my mother? I can no longer touch bottom and, head down, I plow the water in a panicked crawl. I am a new swimmer, a small speck in an infinite ocean and understand how the undertow can sweep you out to sea. And how, if you get too close, you'll be smashed against the sharp boulders of the jetties that mark the beach every twenty metres like a giant ruler. I aim my strokes towards the shore and my mother's olive and white pied umbrella. Another wave hits my back and again I am plowed under. My mother loves the ocean, loves looking at it, drowning her thoughts in it, loves the muscular give of the wet sand against her feet, the sun toasting her skin. In my dream, like in real life, she sits in her beach chair burying her large feet in the warm sand. Behind her large dark glasses she is content, despite not smiling. She doesn't know the danger I'm in. Just doesn't know.

My daughter's small hand on my cheek startles me awake.

"Are you still sick?" she asks. She is holding her slippers, bought at last Saturday's market. They're handmade, silk, a brilliant turquoise trimmed with beadwork. Some of the beads are already missing. I peer past her to the clock. Ten forty. I should get up.

I answer by pulling her up into the bed, tucking her smallness under my chin to rest my head on hers. I close my eyes again.

"I love you, Mommy," she says, burrowing into my chest.

I never know how sincere this cliché is, even from the mouths of babes. And on this of all days, I'm hardly deserving. I have deserted her on the beach. For all I know, the house is on fire.

"Why do you love me?" I ask.

"What?"

"Why do you love me?"

My daughter is inordinately kind to me. My two boys would never have entertained themselves while I slept. I could be throwing up, having a seizure, and they'd start a fight just so I'd have to intervene.

What I expect to hear, even hope to hear from my four-year-old, is more clichés. *Because you're beautiful.*

I could sleep for another hour or two on that one. Or some sort of bribe. *Because you take me to the park. Can we go to the park now, Mommy?*

She takes a minute to think and I start to fade. I tell myself I am going to get up, very, very soon.

"Because," she starts with thoughtful honesty, "I have to love someone."

My heart tightens my chest. She's a child, hard-wired for love. She has to love someone. Can she already have that much sense of her own aloneness? I had no idea.

"Sweetheart," I say, opening my eyes and pulling her face up to meet mine.

Her pink-cheeked face is so animated by my reaction, my breath hinges in my throat before I laugh out loud. She starts to laugh too, her keen eyes lunging into mine.

It's as if we're the same age.

HER BACK TO ME, my mother was bent over her sewing machine. She was making changes, alterations, to an old tweed suit. A suit I hadn't seen her wear for years now.

"I wore them out," I announced casually, as if it was no big deal, all in a day's work.

"Mmm?" She was concentrating on guiding the bumpy material past the stabbing needle. She snorted as it bunched, then wrenched it free. Had she already forgotten about the shoes? About me?

"See?" I thrust them towards her.

She stopped sewing, pushed her glasses up over her hair and turned towards the shoes. She studied the shoes, my face, the shoes. A kind of shocked recognition came over her eyes, as if she'd just now realized who I really was. Standing there in my navy socks waiting for her to speak, I felt suddenly weightless, about to lift off the floor.

She ran one finger over the left shoe's worst damage and her eyes seemed to wobble. Then her face began to melt towards her nose. Her gasp made me jump. A hand flew to her mouth and a strangled cry dragged her out of her chair and pushing past me. My shoes and her sewing both left dangling.

I found her in the bathroom, the door not all the way closed. As silently as I could, I pushed it open. She was sitting on the toilet seat, gulping, a tissue held to her face.

"I'm sorry," was all I knew to say. "I'm really sorry." I'd never seen my mother cry before and felt my own tears coming.

She didn't seem to hear me. A deep injured moan poured out of her. A descending sound, as if something inside her was falling. She pulled a towel off its ring, buried her face, but the moaning continued. I was afraid to let that sound reach bottom. I took a breath and spoke up louder.

"I'm really sorry, Mom."

She glanced up, eyes pink and glittering. She nodded, smiled an embarrassed smile. The awful sound had stopped.

"I didn't mean to..." I was about to say "do it" but that was hardly true "...make you cry."

"It's okay," Mom said between hiccups. "I'm just...tired today."

She turned her head and blew her nose. I could tell she didn't want me watching and I started to leave.

"I'll be out in a minute," she said, and the effort in her voice made my stomach hurt.

"I'll set the table," I said quickly and started to run.

In the kitchen, I wrapped the ruined saddle shoes in a paper bag and stuffed them in the bottom of the garbage. We never said another word about those shoes or her crying. Acted like it never happened.

I GET OUT OF BED, put on my robe and am met by the canine devotee camped outside my door. His mindless tail thumps the wall and he beams up at me, his eyes full of intelligence. Or so it seems. My daughter pats his head, doing my duty.

"I'm hungry again," she says, her eyes on the dog.

"You're always hungry again."

She looks up, eyes grabbing mine.

"Not when I eat something."

I smirk, bend over and pat the dog. Alone and together, my daughter and I head to the kitchen.

Sunday Bastard

POUCHED ON AARON'S BACK IN A NEW STATE-of-the-art kid sack, five-month-old Max is babbling way too close to one ear. Whenever the babble stops, Aaron believes he can hear the brightness of the store's fluorescent lights. He squints at the shelves of tinned fruit, then back at the list in his hand. Wendy was off in the mall, an important baby snowsuit sale, and he'd been left in charge of Max and this list. He reads the first item again: *Mandarin oranges from Taiwan, not China.*

Smelling booze and wondering if it is dribbling out his pores, Aaron turns to find some old guy in a beige raincoat and red toque staring at Max. A large, circular button that says *Jesus Loves Me* is pinned at a rakish angle to the raincoat's lapel. The letter *o* in *Loves* is heart shaped. What about me? thinks Aaron.

"Can I help you?" Aaron offers with a smile. The pains in his skull root deeper. Why isn't the Aspirin working? And why did he drink those cognacs after all that champagne? Last night he and Wendy had christened the house – "Ours!" – breaking (after several tries) a cheap bottle of sparkling against a corner of the garage. Then they opened the real stuff. As a result of his savvy in the stock market, he'd paid off the mortgage and now owned a piece of the earth and the house on it. It was a good feeling, ownership. No, a great feeling. After Max went to bed, he and Wendy had made love in front of the fire. His control freak wife became something softly wild during sex, a lynx or a mink, and uncharacteristically spontaneous. Afterwards, she'd gone to bed, but he'd stayed up and shared a sixty-year-old cognac with Neil Young.

Max grabs a tight fist of Aaron's hair. "Ow, big guy." Aaron gently releases himself. "Please, don't hurt daddy."

The drunk's still gawking. "Sure hope he looks like his mother," he says, and shakes his head in a kind of figure eight.

Aaron forces a laugh and pain spikes through the back of an eye.

The man grunts and walks on.

Whatever, thinks Aaron, and turns his attention back to the rows of canned fruit. He picks up a tin of mandarins and remembers his mother's words when she saw her grandson that first time. *Sure doesn't look like any of my babies.*

"Excuse me," comes a clipped voice, "your cart is blocking the aisle."

"Sorry." Aaron shifts his cart.

Her eyes fixed on her hands, the woman pushes past.

"You're welcome," he mutters, then returns to the can in his hand. Taiwan, reads the label. He drops it in the cart.

Though Max started out with dark hair, that fell out and he turned curiously blond. Really blond. And his baby blues have mutated into a sea green. Nobody on either side has green eyes. Wendy was a blue-eyed brunette and Aaron's hair was even darker, a shade lighter than his eyes. Was Max even genetically feasible? He should ask Dr. Tim on his old-timers team. No: what would such a question imply? He and Wendy have been married only four and some years. It's a good marriage. Extremely good. Last night's romp on the rug attests to that.

Aaron reads: *Spartan mineral water (sodium free), President's Choice rice cakes with millet (unsalted), bananas a touch green...*Jesus.

"Nama, nama, nama," spouts Max.

He reaches behind and gives Max a pat on his chubby leg. "Hang in there." He checks his watch. Twenty minutes before he's to meet Wendy at the checkout. A half hour is normally Max's limit without his nama. "We'll see mama soon, little buddy."

Aaron avoids saying Max. Doesn't care for the name. Wendy calls their son "Maxey." Makes him think of maxi-pad. His boy was born the day the Great One played his last game and Aaron wanted to call him Wayne. The little spitter looked just like a

Wayne. Everyone had a kid called Max these days. Wendy, though, found great comfort in trends. She could tell a car's year by colour alone and owned the same clothes actors were wearing on TV. Max's new snowsuit will probably be silver blue to match their new Matrix. Aaron pushes on a thorn under his eyebrow. Fuck, his head hurts.

At the wall of rice cakes there are three, no four brands, but none with millet. Maybe she slipped off to the sperm bank after their three years of trying. Isn't there definitive blood testing you can do? He sees the old drunk over in dairy slip a pound of butter inside his raincoat. Jesus love you now? He hopes the guy gets caught.

Down the cereal aisle, Gretzky's picture smiles out from a box of Cheerios.

"My boy, Wayne," he says, holding up the box for Max to swat at. Though not on the list, he chucks it in the cart.

Oatmeal, large flake, not Quakers. He grabs the first bag that meets his hand. Wendy, relax already.

He always thought Wendy'd be less controlling if she were larger. She was petite, five-foot-one, her figure already exercised back to its size 5 wardrobe. Her shoulder-length hair with the dead-even bangs, reminded him of a soft samurai helmet. Aaron was six-two and had to hunch to kiss her. His wife needed things a certain way at a certain time, which was the source of her vulnerability, and her strength. With no patience for surprises, zero tolerance for variables, she had to know all her Christmas, birthday and anniversary presents ahead of time. She refused to see a movie she hadn't seen the trailer for, had chosen her job for its pension plan and had so many ultrasounds when pregnant that the doctor cut her off. But...if this child was, say, his buddy Charlie's, or that new hotshot lawyer's in her office – what's his name? – then she'd be racked with genetic unknowns...which is maybe why she had all those...

He locates the mineral water, reads the price and refuses to buy it. Drink it out of the tap like the rest of us. Max begins to whimper and Aaron jiggles the pack, shoulders crimping at the thought of a wailing baby on his back. He digs in his coat for the rubber caterpillar Wendy gave him for emergencies.

"Okay, big guy?" he says, handing back the toy. "Chew on this."

Come on, he pleads, take it. Ten minutes to go. Max takes the caterpillar, squeezing out a sickly squeak, and Aaron's headache begins an even pulsing behind both eyes. He pictures cartoon eyes bugging out of his head to a disco rhythm. Then he steps on something that screams at him. The neon green rubber caterpillar is belly up on the linoleum floor. He bends to pick it up and blood hurtles dangerously to his head. Her old boyfriend, Richard, is blond. As blond as Max. Richard Kurtz. Aaron took to calling him Dick behind his back. Dick Kurtz. She never really got over Dick, the pilot, who flies into town every third week or so. With a firm grip on the cart, he carefully rights himself, blows on the bug and hands it back to Max.

"Do you think that's sanitary?" A young woman is scrunching her nose at him. Her hair's a freak show of curls, and hip red glasses ride low on her nose. His head hurts too much to answer.

It's a relief to escape the narrow centre aisles into the expanse of produce, yet his mouth is so dry he's finding it hard to swallow. His brain is dehydrated, probably half its normal size and he wishes he'd grabbed some of Wendy's fancy water after all.

There's the old man again, on the far side of the banana table. He's slipping an apple, two, down the deep outside pocket of his coat. God, what else has he planted on himself? Aaron picks out a yellow bunch with brown spots. I happen to prefer ripe bananas, Wendy.

"Filling up with food, are we?" asks Aaron.

The guy glances up with eyes that barely register Aaron, eyes that could care less, then he moves along to the oranges.

Aaron looks around the corners of the ceiling. Don't they have security cameras in this place? Is this guy really getting away with this? He's so obvious. Is it the Jesus button? No one dares suspect the Jesus guy. Maybe it's equally obvious that Max isn't really his. Maybe all those fatherhood jokes in the dressing room were actually directed at him.

"Don't even think about sex after baby."

"Just make sure there was sex before." Fart-releasing guffaws.

Both their plumbing had checked out just fine. "*Armies of sperm, a basketful of eggs, clear egg hoops,*" the funny man specialist had told them. But after two-and-a-half years of temperature taking and factory-timed sex, Wendy had been pretty frustrated. He remembers one crying jag, holding her in bed, her small fist pounding his chest and the yellow bruise it left over his heart. Her clock was set and she couldn't take the unpredictability of it all. The next day she had talked about going the in vitro route but, knowing how her friend Sandy had suffered, never pursued it. Funny how she was pregnant not long after that final option was dismissed. Pregnant and so happy, both of us. But did they even have sex that month? Fuck, wasn't he in Toronto during March's "window of fertility"? He'll check the dates with his secretary.

He wheels out of produce and scouts the shortest checkout line. Max's whimpers now border on desperation. It's as if Max can smell her coming. He looks at his watch. Another three minutes. Aaron jiggles the pack. He knows that in his mother's arms, Max will instantly quiet. Maybe the fact that he can't soothe his own son is another sign. Maybe there's a pheromone thing that recognizes its own kind.

His headache extends beyond him now to include the tabloid stars caged in magazine racks, the waft of friendly chit-chat, the dull beep, beep, beep of items being scanned. Waiting to unload his cart, he notices the old drunk one checkout over, in the nine-items-or-less aisle. There are four items in his red basket. Probably ten more in his coat, thinks Aaron. He pans for a security guard, those idle shoppers who never accumulate any groceries. There's a guy by the exit door, hands jammed in the pockets of a black zippered jacket. He's wearing a ball cap and looking idle enough. Could be he's waiting to stop the guy just outside the store, avoid a scene.

Wendy comes through the automatic door, a bundle of smart cuteness. Who could resist her? She sees him, smiles and waves. He feels his breath let go. No, he thinks, it's alright. We're alright. "Aren't we, spitter," he whispers over his shoulder. "Look, there's your —"

At the sight of Wendy, Max lets go a shriek in Aaron's ear that feels like permanent damage.

"Hi, sweetie," she says to Aaron, "I found a great suit for Maxey. In maroon but what can you do?" Aaron bends nearly in half to let Wendy undo the Kidpack's safety strap and lift Max out.

"Here," she instructs him, "take my purse. My discount card's in the front pocket. I'll go feed Maxey."

Wendy takes Max to the bench under the front windows, discreetly unhooks her nursing bra and slips Max's already puckered up mouth under her shirt. A flash of pale skin and he's on, her shirt draping his cheek. Aaron unloads his items onto the counter. The drunk with his measly bag of groceries is starting towards the security guy at the door, his backside protruding under his coat as if a side of ham's shoved down his pants. Under the shadow of his visor, the security guy is looking right past the guy. What? Security is staring at his wife's tit.

"You have a discount card today, sir?"

"What?"

"Your discount card? Have you signed up for one yet?"

"Yeah," Aaron looks down at the purse in his hands. "It's my wife's, in here somewhere."

He removes her wallet. It holds a dozen cards but no Superstore card. Looking from the guard to Wendy and back to the purse, he pulls out tissues, comb, mirror, lipstick, green Tic Tacs, baby wipes, piling them on the counter.

"It's green," says the clerk, suppressing a smile.

The drunk is walking right past Security.

"Hey," Aaron yells at no one in particular. Wendy and the security guard simultaneously turn in his direction. The drunk glances over his shoulder, then continues out of the store.

"Is there a problem?" asks the clerk.

Wendy has put her sucked and ogled breast away and is striding over.

"Aaron, the card's not in my wallet," she says, seeing half her purse strewn over the counter. "Give me my bag." She holds out her hand.

"No." Aaron jerks the bag away, surprising even himself, and the rest of its contents spill onto the person's groceries behind his.

Max starts an obscenely high-pitched cry that makes Aaron swoon, before he spies Wendy's pink diaphragm case astride his neighbour's eggplant. What the...? He lunges for it and hoists it in the air.

"Dick Kurtz!"

The security guy, no longer idle, is at the end of the checkout. "Watch the language, buddy."

"Buddy?" Aaron nearly spits.

"What is wrong with you?" hisses Wendy. "And where's my mineral water?"

"I don't care about your fancy water," Aaron hisses back. He slaps down the pink case. "I care about why you're carrying this around everywhere you go."

Wendy has gone rigid, her eyes boring into his. "Apparently you forgot what we did last night?" She is no longer whispering and her face is flushing pink. "And that I went over to Jan's early this morning to help her choose colours for her kitchen and had to remove it there –"

"Let's go, please," says the woman in line behind him.

There are tears of mortification in his wife's eyes as she turns and walks away, Max's blond arms clinging to her neck. The automated door opens for her and she's gone.

The sound of his own breathing plunges back and forth in his head. His hand shakes as he removes the green card from the pocket of Wendy's empty, flaccid bag. He hands it to the cashier, who will no longer meet his eye. He glances around. Blond men, black-haired men, gray heads, even security guy are all avoiding his eye. They sympathize, Aaron tells himself, they've been here. He takes a breath. With a couple more Aspirin, tomorrow he'll be back on top.

Medium Security

COW-TIRED IN ROUTINE, PRISONER 87 STRUTS her stuff down the wrong hall towards the gym entrance. What d'you know, it's the hall where the visiting ballet company is warming up. She high-steps the landmine of limbs crisscrossing the floor. There's a new scent in the air...face powder, and she draws it in like oxygen, remembers when her hair was long enough to make a noose. Remembers again why she lives with one set of prison issue smells. A crime of passion, a bad decision hitched with fraying rope around a waning moon. She was young, innocent until proven otherwise.

Principal Dancer notes the one-woman audience coming down the hall. Black hair, butch cut, a widow's peak like the clawed imprint of a bird. Principal Dancer splits her legs to form an unbroken line from pointed toe to pointed toe. She stretches her torso impossibly forward until her belly presses the cold cement. She's showing off, giving the blue-shirted woman a pre-show, wetting her own lips. She too has committed crimes. Crimes of privilege, of orthodontists, of having to be careful what to wish for. The woman comes closer. Was pretty, thinks Principal Dancer, once upon a time. She wishes she had the woman's nose.

Prisoner 87 wears a pair of prison-issue sneakers, grey tops, red erasers for soles. They stop beside Principal Dancer's long blonde neck. The way the upturned ear curls around itself makes her think of a fetus made of translucent porcelain. Fragile, she thinks. Do not shake.

Principal Dancer smells stale cigarettes and sits up, posture all hype and royalty. Rotating her feet like drunken puppets, she tosses her criminal audience a polished smile. It lands in indifferent eyes. She will have to work harder to win over this one. She watches the woman walk towards the stage door, left arm swinging, the right perfectly silent. It looks like two people share one body.

Armed guards block the gym's entrances and exits. Their cinched belts create waists where there are none. The stage is marked off on the gym floor with black tape, and only a strip of bland wood, six feet wide and the width of an ocean, separates it from bleachers of blue-shirted women loud with recess, women anticipating the next meal, pondering apple, orange, or banana. Each has a number stamped on a useful pocket and each spends hours alone, deciphering her assigned numerology, hoping to break the code and reveal what her future really holds.

Tiny wrap skirts, ivory bodysuits, pink tights, hair pulled to sealskin gloss, eight girls position themselves under the crude gymnasium lights, each having adjusted her makeup accordingly. For luck, each has spit on her toe shoe ribbons before knotting them at the soft spot on the inside of her ankle. Their toes have already begun to bleed.

The lights dim. Bach's Double Violin Concerto in E Minor steals out of the speakers and swallows the talk. Prisoner 87 stops gnawing her hangnail to listen. A new sound in the air. Violins. One and then another. This sound is the fine knife of her own longing. It slips under the toughened layers of skin. The hushed ceiling draws down around her ears and the floor beneath her thick-soled shoes turns to ash.

Enter an Ornamental Male carrying Principal Dancer, glorious, above the heads of the other dancers. His are the only male arms for miles, and miles, and miles. Prisoner 87 leans forward for a better look. His the only male arms for two years, twenty weeks, and fifteen thousand days. A rumble of awe as those smooth, muscled arms lower Principal Dancer onto the soundless tip of one satin toe. With her eyes, Prisoner 87 licks the narrow sideburns of sweat that roll down his temples.

Principal Dancer strokes the music towards the blue blur of shirts. She hurries, bends, turns, leaps, never falters, and invisible Male hands are there to catch her, there to catch her, there to catch her. Her pared-down breasts, more muscle than flesh, heave with each timed breath. She believes she is the envy of every woman here.

Prisoner 87 breathes through a mouth that won't stay closed. Bach's violins meet and separate, sneak under and around, teasing out promises, promises strung with desire, then doubt, fury, a frenzy of regret. His arms hold Principal Dancer as she arcs back and back, her spine threatening to snap. Prisoner 87 leans her head back and back, her eyes squeezing shut. A shared violin note rips high.

"Kiss her," Prisoner 87 cries at the stage, the crack in her voice swallowing an ocean. "Kiss me," she hisses into a riot of whistles, of so many red-soled shoes thrumming the bleacher steps.

Principal Dancer leans toward the Ornamental Male, only the muscle of her heart missing a beat. Prisoner 87 cradles her face in her hands, and remembers.

The Cult of Quick Repair

J ANET HANGS UP THE PHONE, BREATHING HARD
through her mouth as if she's been climbing stairs.
Hospice is on their way. She tries to take a deep
breath. There are too many people and not enough
oxygen in her mother's cottage-sized house, she
thinks irritably.

God, she wants to fling open the doors and windows, let the cold billow the curtains, scatter the dust,
bring this deadly wait to a quicker end. No, no, sorry
Mom, she doesn't mean it. She takes an almond canoe
from the open package on the counter, eats it just to
have something else to focus on for a minute. She
doesn't even like the taste, but the dense, chewy tex-
ture feels good in her mouth.

Movement out the kitchen window catches her eye.
Squirrels, no doubt. Yep, two squirrels chasing each
other around the trunk of a Douglas fir. Her mother's
forested garden consists of fir and cedar trees, plus one

peeling arbutus, which enclose a small green rectangle of lawn that's more moss than grass. At the garden's far end is an inlaid brick patio and freestanding fireplace. Her generous, outgoing mother liked to entertain and such evenings always wound up outside by the fire with pots of tea and her almond canoes, maybe a snifter of Bailey's Irish Cream. Tucked in on the right, positioned on a old stump, is her mother's Buddha. The size of a preteen, he's sitting in meditation, eyes closed, just a hint of a smile. His moss-covered back makes it look like he's wearing a shiny green cape. Superbuddha.

Janet has slept at her mom's every night for the last six weeks, stopping by her apartment on her way to work for a change of clothes. After work she comes directly here and each night, after dinner, her bedridden mother has asked her to place an "offering" on the statue's lap: a piece of fruit sometimes, but usually an almond canoe: her mother's favourite cookie.

"An offering to what?" Janet asked that first night.

"Well, I guess, to the things we can't see, can't know," answered her mom, sounding unsure. "I tend to think of them as my angels. Buddhists would call them local deities or protectors."

"What happened to believing in plain old God?" God, at least when Janet was growing up, used to be the operative word. Though not particularly religious about it, their family did attend the local Anglican church back when, and Janet had always considered herself a Christian.

"Sure. Him too. And Mrs. God." Her mother smiled her impish smile. "But really it just feels like

I'm offering up my smaller, more limited mind to meld with something bigger. I shouldn't really even give It a name because that limits It again."

Janet shook her head but wasn't going to argue with a dying woman. And she could understand how one might get superstitious near the end, hedge one's bets. So every night she slipped her feet into her mother's old gardening boots and walked across the spongey moss lawn to balance an offering in the statue's cold, conveniently flat, sandstone palms. His palms are laid one on top of the other, thumbs raised to make a little curved archway. Those empty hands look to her like they've been just waiting patiently all day for the handout. Sometimes, out there alone in the dark, she'd get a little spooked and imagine its heavy eyelids rising and those tapered stone fingers snapping closed over hers, tired of almond canoes and wanting her as the offering. Human flesh.

By morning the food would have been stolen by any number of squirrels who, as a result, now populated the yard and came far too close to the house for comfort.

She walks back into the cramped living room where her dying mom, bald as a baby, eyes closed despite being awake, lies inert on a hospital bed in front of the couch. Somber Uncle Phil sits in a chair holding his sister's hand and Janet's brother, Silas, who finally deigned to show up yesterday, paces because he has zero capacity for stillness. Though she hasn't seen him for half a year, his habits annoy her as much as ever.

Filling the couch are three people she never laid eyes on until this afternoon. Mom had actually requested to be displayed like this in the living room, saying her bedroom was too small to accommodate both family and her "family of buddhas," as she called them, who came in organized shifts from nine in the morning until nine at night. "The atmosphere of meditation will help me let go," her mother had said.

Again, who was Janet to argue, but she can't get past her own irritation to experience any "atmosphere" emanating from these *buddha teams* as she thinks of them. Every fifteen minutes, the man on the couch, whose name is Henry, rises out of his place on the couch to lean into Mom's ear and whisper a string of foreign-sounding syllables. No other team member has done this ritual. Mom repeats the syllables after him. It feels like they're keeping a secret from Janet and it pisses her off. On the other hand, does she even want to know?

Mom moans a sustained nasal moan, and Janet feels the tiny muscles around her eyes tightening.

"Hospice is on their way," she says plainly, matter-of-factly. She doesn't know how else to says things in front of strangers. Their eyes may be closed but their ears aren't. Actually, the Henry fellow has his eyes open slightly yet focused on nothing. He looks like a zombie.

Mom manages a barely perceptible nod to show she understands, and Silas stops his pacing to nod briskly, his round eyes shiny gray dimes. He's chewed a bright red colour into his lips. She knows that Silas slept as little as she did last night, yet somehow he has sparks coming off him. She wonders what he's on besides the pot of coffee he drank earlier. Silas, twenty-four, is three years her junior. His shoulder-length hair looks greasy despite a morning shower. Probably used the conditioner by mistake. He'd be a handsome guy, thinks Janet, if he wasn't so gaunt and actually took care of himself.

"They're on their way," Uncle Phil repeats close to Mom's ear. "I've got to go but I'll drop back over after my shift." He kisses her fingers where they curve around his, then places her hand on top of her swollen belly.

Henry clears his throat and Uncle Phil looks over at him with cold hatred.

"Goddamn strangers," mutters Uncle Phil, turning his head so only Janet hears.

"Mystic vigilantes" is what Silas called them last night. "Get it, vigil-aunties?"

Janet thinks of them as voyeurs, here to witness the big spiritual climax of death.

"Bye, Uncle Phil," says Janet, "I'll call you if..."

"The angels come," Mom whispers through teeth too heavy to part.

Janet smiles and Uncle Phil shakes his head sadly. Two beats late, Silas barks out a laugh.

"Her mind's all there," says Silas, grinning, his voice too bright for this moment.

Janet kisses her uncle's cheek then takes his place beside Mom and across from the buddha team, Henry and two women. A grey-haired woman, who's dressed in jeans and turtleneck, is using Mom's nicest pillow, the gold Persian one with silk fringe, under her bum as she sits cross-legged on the couch. The other, a young woman in an expensive-looking suit, sits with her stocking feet planted on the floor and Mom's antique satin pillows propping her back. Eyes closed, she clicks what resembles a rosary without a cross between thumb and forefinger, her silent lips moving like a taste tester forgetting to swallow. Janet can sense their awareness sticking out into the room, taking everything in, including the limited oxygen. Though silent, they feel glaringly present and she resents it. Billowing ferns, spider plants and Christmas cacti in pink bloom fill the bay window behind them. From where Janet's sits, Henry looks like he's wearing one dripping pink earring on his left ear. She can remember Henry's name since it's the name of her boyfriend's cat, but can't for the life of her remember the ladies' names. Again Henry leans forward and mumbles his gobbledygook in Mom's ear. Mom mumbles back. It looks like brainwashing the weak.

Six years ago, not long after Dad left her for the proverbial younger woman, Mom began spending every Tuesday evening and at least one weekend a month meditating with this group and studying Buddhism. Janet never really understood her mother's connection to these seemingly brooding intellectual types, but her mom said meditation enabled her to "let go of those things she couldn't change."

But to this day Janet believes Mom's illness is a direct result of these pacifying attitudes, repressing her anger toward Dad. Janet, though, is still angry enough for the both of them. After twenty-two years of marriage to a person as generous and self-sacrificing as Mom, his "falling in love" was not an excuse. Janet cannot, will not, forgive him and hasn't spoken to him for five years now.

A week ago, Mom asked Janet to contact him for her, to tell him she was dying. "I'm glad to know he has someone else. I really am. And I want him to know, just in case he has any regrets and wants to say goodbye." Janet said she would, but had no intention of doing it. Her plan was to call him after the fact, shock him, she hoped, force him to experience the same degree of loss and confusion he'd put Mom through. In fact, in a morbid way, she was even looking forward to it.

Another pitiful moan and Mom rolls her head from side to side. Her restlessness had started late last night and Janet hardly slept, worrying that this might be it. And now she's got Silas here to worry about. Silas, the x in any equation, feels like an accident waiting to happen. Janet squeezes her mother's hand and feels the weak effort in return.

Mom struggles to pull her knobby knees up under the covers, in order to turn onto her side. Even with the extra pain medication, she can't seem to get comfortable. If only these buddha people weren't around, she'd try and distract Mom with music maybe — what's so holy about silence anyway? — or those anti-Bush jokes that were going around a while back. Her mom had loved the one about Bush in a restaurant ordering the "quickie." The waitress gets indignant, walks away, then Cheney explains to Bush how to pronounce "quiche." Janet smiles at the memory, can almost hear Mom's infectious belly laugh.

Mom plucks weakly at her covers.

"Silas," Janet says. "Help me here, please."

Silas smiles, baring his teeth. His teeth are so white, she wonders if there's some chemical in his saliva that acts like bleach. It takes him several seconds to unstick his feet from his piece of carpet. Janet knows it's hard for him, a shock really, to see how much Mom's changed these last six months, the amount of weight she's lost, the loss of her wavy mane of hair.

"Other side of the bed, Silas, and take her shoulders," Janet instructs with her chin.

Silas tentatively moves to the other side and rubs his hands up and down on the thighs of his jeans. Then he holds his hands up in the air like a surgeon awaiting his gloves.

"Just do it," she says. Grow up is what she wants to say.

"He's an artist. He's sensitive," her mother would say. He's self-absorbed is Janet's perspective.

Eyes squinting, as if afraid something might come off in his hand, Silas gently turns his mother's shoulders while Janet guides her hips and knees. The buddha team continue with their respective meditating and bead counting. Janet has to wonder if Mom started gagging, flailing or worse, if these three would even react or simply meditate and mumble all the harder.

"Okay, good," breathes Silas after Mom is safely settled on her side. He backs up and into one of the meditators on the couch. "Oh shit, sorry," he says to rosary woman. "I mean ship, no, shoot. Your foot okay?"

"Fine," she mumbles through a smile, not bothering to open her eyes. She readjusts her pillows and fidgets an inch backwards. Henry leans forwards and mumbles into Mom's ear. Mom mumbles back. Go away, thinks Janet.

Silas escapes into the kitchen. Janet hears rummaging in the fridge and calls to him to put on the kettle for the hospice people, due anytime now. Janet has, upon each new buddha team's arrival, offered them tea and almond canoes, because she knows that's what Mom would do. She uses Mom's favourite red teapot, the Matisse mugs and the sunflower "cookie plate."

"Okay, sure," he calls over the sound of something falling.

Silas took the boat over yesterday morning from Vancouver, days later than he'd promised. Mom had held on for him. Two minutes after he walked in the door, she took his face in her palms and performed a wearied version of her ritual kissing of both cheeks followed by his forehead. Then she smiled and shut her eyes. It was as if his face was the final thing her eyes needed to see, because she hasn't opened them since.

Much to Janet's dismay, Mom was still sending him a monthly allowance because his "art" didn't yet make ends meet.

"It only goes up his nose or up in smoke," Janet told her. "One or the other."

"Silas does things his way, Janet," Mom would say gently, as if far more concerned with Janet's ungenerous attitude.

Janet wouldn't call him an addict, not yet, just a hard-core partier, hungry for anything other than reality. She remembers his model car phase at age ten. How he locked himself in his room, taking weeks to build one stupid car, the air in there nothing but glue fumes. When he was sixteen it was spray-paint art. He even got good enough to sell to tourists down in the Victoria Harbour; Silas the only spray artist not wearing a gas mask. Since dropping out of art school, he's turned to sealing objects in acrylic. Dried flowers, pasta, watch parts, Disney toys, preserved forever in Future floor wax and sold as paperweights, soap dishes, kitchen tiles, even tabletops. Mom had thought it might be fun to commission a kitchen floor of almond canoes.

"Would make for a lovely colour really. That warm gold." They'd imagined walls and furniture, an entire house of embalmed food. Had a good laugh.

It's devastating to Janet that her mom's laugh is now lost to the world. She should have recorded it, she tells herself, should have made a tape loop to play whenever something funny happened. Like the canned laughter on sitcoms. She could put it on right now, see if the buddha team would react. People used to say that Silas had Mom's laugh. It's similar, Janet admits, but phony in comparison, the sound without the substance. Silas can't settle into his body long enough to laugh like Mom. He's too hungry, always one step ahead of his skin.

A soft knocking at the door and Janet calls to Silas to answer it.

"What?" calls Silas.

"Get the door."

"I didn't even hear the door," Silas says, coming out of the kitchen.

"Just get it."

Mom presses Janet's hand. "He's listening for angels," she breathes.

No, he's not, thinks Janet, squeezing back. She has no sympathy for Silas. He hasn't been the one driving to specialists, chemo treatments, cooking meals, spending overnights. And he isn't the one with the full-time job and boyfriend.

Janet cringes as she listens to Silas's disjointed greeting.

"Hi. Welcome. Good of you to come. I'm the son."

The son of what? God?

"We're in here," she calls.

"Yeah, this way," says Silas.

The social worker introduces herself as Eve. She's tall, forty-five maybe, with cropped black hair and eyes like a whiskey jack's. The younger woman, Martha, is the nurse. Framed by shoulder-length blonde hair, Martha's pretty face is more practical than anything, her expression like those of the men and women on the Texas Hold'em channel Janet's boyfriend sometimes watches. Martha carries a large black tackle box which she hoists onto the dining room table.

Eve does the talking. Her voice is calm and confident, upbeat even. No holy silence for her. She makes it sound as if helping people die is the best job ever. She instantly makes Janet feels less alone. And less afraid for her mother.

"My angels?" mumbles Mom.

"Yes, your angels have arrived," says Janet, and Eve laughs a free, unselfconscious laugh.

"I'm Eve, Lorna," she says, kneeling beside Mom and placing a firm hand on her forehead. "We're here to make you as comfortable as possible."

This sounds slightly sinister to Janet. *Angels of death* she'd like to say, thinking Mom would laugh at that if she could.

"I hurt," says Mom. Above her closed eyes, her smooth brow crinkles slightly.

"I know," says Eve. "It's all right."

"How are *you* holding out?" Eve has turned her friendly bird-eyes on Janet.

"Me?" Janet stutters at the question. "Well, I really can't complain, considering." She glances down at her mom.

Eve nods warmly, knowingly. "So tell me, how's she been today?"

"She still won't open her eyes. Hasn't slept much, if at all, in the last twenty-four hours. She's been very restless, can't seem to get comfortable."

"The restlessness is very common at this stage," Eve says. "The dying feel like there's someplace they need to get to. The body's anticipating the journey."

This plain talk about death makes Janet instantly angry. Not angry at her mother for dying, but angry at herself for wanting it to be true, wanting it to be over and done already.

"I've seen people pack a suitcase," says Eve, smiling.

Janet doesn't want to hear about other people. "So what happens now?"

"Well," Eve speaks to Mom's closed eyes, "Martha will administer some morphine and a little Ativan, to help your body relax, Lorna, and then a third needle to prevent hemorrhaging."

Afraid that this new stage of things might be a little too real for Silas, Janet looks over to see him standing in the kitchen doorway, furtively sipping a Coke. She doesn't remember hearing the kettle boil. He probably forgot to plug it in. Janet follows his gaze to where Martha has opened her tackle box, packed with row upon row of little vials. Martha lifts out three and taps their glass with her fingernail. Three syringes follow and a whip of tan rubber tubing.

"Silas," Janet's voice is abrupt. "Is the tea ready?"

"Oh, the tea." He ducks back into the kitchen.

She sighs. Maybe she should just go ahead and put on some of Mom's favourite music – Tom Jones or Barbara. She's about to ask her mother if she'd like that when she speaks first.

"You called Robbie?" breathes Mom, as she turns herself onto her back with a slight thud. "Called your dad?"

"Yes," Janet says quickly.

Her mother's lips part with a huff, the sound of grief, of being abandoned all over again. Her chin falls towards her chest. No, wait. Janet doesn't want her to feel like that. Should she call him now? Force him to come? But he lives an hour north. If he's even home, that is.

Martha is there, holding three prepared syringes on a small napkin-covered tray.

"We'll need one arm, Lorna," says Eve, "and one shot we'll put in your leg."

Mom slowly lifts her chin. "Yes."

"Can Martha sit there for this, Janet?" Eve indicates the chair.

"Oh, sure." She stands. "But...how much time do we have after..." She strains to see the clock on the kitchen wall. Silas waves at her from the kitchen doorway. "Tea's on," he mouths.

"We can't really say."

"Will this..." She wants to say kill her but that won't sound right.

"She'll still be aware, but not so responsive." Eve has obviously answered this question before.

The first needle pierces her mother's flesh.

Oh god, should she call Dad? But she hasn't spoken to him in five years. Or maybe she should tell Mom the truth. But then she'd have to explain why she never called him, and can't really, with these people around. In the quiet, Janet can hear the gray-haired woman's deep breathing moving in and out behind her. In and out. It's a soothing, uncomplicated sound, and for a moment that's all there is.

"There, that wasn't so bad, was it?" says Martha, picking up the next needle.

Mom sighs in response. Henry stands and leans over in Mom's ear again. Mom mumbles back.

Janet once asked her mom if she was sure this group wasn't some sort of cult. Mom looked a little taken aback by the word cult. "No, it isn't, because they're not offering a quick fix. Buddhism is concerned with the root cause of suffering. Why we suffer. Why we're never satisfied with these moments of our lives."

"Because God's a jerk?" Janet had said cynically, but her mom hadn't laughed.

The word cult had obviously stung a little because a week later, she and Mom were watching television together when she used it again. Viagra commercials had been playing in between shows, graying men being affectionate towards their creased-faced wives. "The dick fix," she'd snorted, making Janet laugh. "This modern world has become the cult of quick repair," she'd added with a tsk.

Janet felt that, in her roundabout way, Mom was referring to Dad, and was glad to see her letting off a little steam. Which made her think that, yes, she should probably call him now. Or should she?

The second needle slips into her mother's thigh and Janet turns to see Silas setting the tea tray on the dining table. Then comes the third needle, which is inserted in the neck. Janet can't look. Silas has gone into the front hall, is putting on his coat. She goes over to him.

"I got to go for a walk," he says, smiling nervously.

"I understand," she says and means it. "Be back soon though, huh?"

"Oh, yeah. Don't worry."

She steps close to him and hugs him. He feels so thin, and so stiff. It's like hugging a piece of wood but she holds on. He pats her tentatively on the back in return.

"Do you think I should tell Dad she's dying?" whispers Janet, pulling away.

"He doesn't know?" he asks.

"I didn't tell him, did you?"

"Was I supposed to?"

"No, no, but do you think I should call him now?"

"Yeah, he should probably know."

"Could you call him?" she asks. "It's been like five −"

"I really want to go out now," he says, an eager hand on the door. "I'll call him when I get back."

"Okay. Or maybe I'll just do it." She watches him leave, surprised to see that it's nearly dark outside. She hadn't thought it was that late.

When she returns to the living room, Eve is in the chair beside Mom taking her pulse. Mom is snoring lightly; finally she's asleep. Or is she dying? It's too late to call now. She couldn't wake her up. She'll wait until Silas returns and then see. The buddha team is perfectly still, the suited woman no longer mumbling and handling her beads. Janet goes to the tray on the dining table and pours herself a cup of tea, picks up an almond canoe. All she's eaten today are these damn things.

"Eve, can you help me look?" Martha is leaning over her tackle box. "I seem to be missing a couple morphine vials."

"Oh?"

"Unless I counted wrong."

What? Oh, god, thinks Janet. Silas. Eve comes over and gets down on her hands and knees to comb through the thick pile carpet. Janet closes her eyes, pictures her brother squatting under a tree some-where, tying off his arm. Mom hiccups in her sleep, a softly goofy sound that makes Janet laugh out loud. It's too much. It's all too much.

"Excuse me," she says and puts down her tea. She makes her way to the kitchen door, slips on her mother's gardening boots. Cookie in hand, she goes outside. To make an offering.

Fireworks

BECCA OPENS HER EYES TO FIND NOEL propped up beside her, quietly reading. She remembers last night and shuts them again. Another new position and another failed attempt. One of her ribs is sore on the left side. Rubbing it, she remembers Uncle Tony and quickly looks at the bedside clock. Nearly eleven.

"It's late." She throws off the duvet.

"He's not going anywhere," Noel chimes from behind his book.

"No, but he prefers visiting before lunch." She pulls on her bra and yesterday's underwear, then slips into her pale yellow dress. "Where are my sandals?"

"You're not going to shower?" Noel sounds alarmed.

"No time." Her uncle wouldn't notice or care.

"Do give him my regards and tell him I'm crazy in love with his niece."

She lengthens out across the bed, a slender bridge, and they kiss. "Me too."

Before climbing into her car, Becca sees Noel in his navy and white striped robe, waving from the upstairs window. His hand cups the air and twists gently side to side like the Queen's. She wonders if it's an English thing. Noel is from Nottingham, home of Robin Hood, holds a doctorate from Cambridge. She blows a kiss, he catches it up in a quick fist and gives his knuckles a slow, drawn-out lick. She forces a laugh but is uneasy at the sight of his tongue.

Pulling out of the drive she thinks how she loves Noel's orderly little house with its apple red door, the primitive African figures, his alphabetized CD collection, the curry smell oozing from the walls. Noel is the youngest full professor in UNB's biology department, where Becca is doing her masters and teaching a 100 class. At thirty-seven, he is ten years her senior. A perfect age difference, in her opinion. He's handsome and well-liked; in short, he's a prize. So what in hell is she going to do?

As much as she desperately wants to and as hard as Noel tries, she just can't get there. Since falling in love a year ago, she fears Noel's jaw has grown noticeably larger, like ball players with a gum chewing habit, his speech even crisper. These changes, she believes, are the result of increasingly lengthy oral calisthenics performed for her benefit. It isn't that his technique is poor – he could have sent thousands of women into grace by now – it's just that when her muscles start to ignite one by one from that tiny match head, slowly subsuming her reasoning mind, threatening to contort her entire being into some snarling gargoyle...she shuts down. Because to make it to the top of that mountain, to make it over that cliff for whatever lay beyond, she can feel and just knows that she'd have to shed all feminine mystique and huff like cattle, pump like a dog, strain, sweat, maybe even swear as she disfigures into a person so wholly unattractive Noel, or any decent man for that matter, would be frightened away. Especially Noel, whose own orgasms arrive quickly, with apparent ease, the only change in his demeanor a gasping open of his eyes as if he's been shot in the back.

Becca knows that men are attracted to her tapered wrists and ankles. They exclaim over her mole-less skin, "so uniform," and her remarkable lack of scent. Noel says she has hair the colour of creamed corn. He commends her speech as "lyrical for a Canadian," says she has a ballerina's carriage. They have everything in common; a passion for reading sediment plugs, canoeing and watching tennis on TV. They love to entertain for four, discover new sparkling whites and rosés, watch foreign comedies. They even share a penchant for black licorice, more than once incorporating the laces and twizzlers into their lovemaking. (She could play, she just couldn't win.)

But Noel feels it's imperative, if they are to marry, that he be able to bring her, as he once called it, "to the ultimate abandon of love."

She pulls up to a stoplight. "As if my not coming makes him any less a man," she says crossly, "or me any less a woman."

She continues up Regent Street. With her previ-
ous two lovers, sex was deemed a success as long as he
came. The man, after all, risks physical injury doesn't
he? She's always enjoyed the sensations she has during
sex, the glittery nerves, the heat and thump of it all,
and just assumed that one day, with the right man,
orgasm would just happen, not unlike a sneeze.

"I want to, I really do," she says as she changes
lanes to turn left.

This Saturday is the anniversary of their "first
time" and Noel will, undoubtedly, be armed with
expectations. She blames his time in India and that
religion of fantastic positions, the Kama Sutra, as having ruined sex for the ordinary person. "Well," she
huffs, turning into visitor parking, "either I learn to
fake it or figure out just how in heck to traverse that
last ugly mile." She snorts a laugh. "Who'm I kidding?
I could never fake it. Can't even tell a lie without
stuttering." I'm just going to have to man-up, she tells
herself, recalling one of her uncle's favourite expres-
sions.

Uncle Tony was Becca's favourite adult when
growing up. Becca was an only child and her parents,
both academics (sociology), were fastidious, indoor
types. Uncle Tony, her mother's brother, was the one
who took her fishing, gave her death-defying pushes
on the rope swing and, when her parents weren't
around to disapprove, suspended her upside down
while subjecting her to the hysterics of tickle tor-
tures. She fishes her credit card from her purse. Poor
Uncle Tony.

As she steps off the elevator, the heels of her sandals are shameless against the linoleum and she tip-toes the rest of the way to her uncle's room. A cart loaded with blood-filled vials is blocking the door-way. Blood's really more maroon than red, Becca notes before a nurse pops up on the cart's other side and startles her.

"Are you a relation?" accuses the woman, her face careless and flat.

"I'm his niece," Becca enunciates in the English accent she's practiced with Noel. "I have brought him some things he has requested." She's watched time and again the change in people after hearing Noel speak. As if the ability to elicit one's consonants displayed a superior intellect, a more favoured birth. Twice he'd crisp talked his way out of a speeding ticket.

"Oh...all right, dear," the bossy eyes suddenly less sure. "He's just resting now. Go on in."

The woman wheels away and Becca tiptoes over to where her uncle lies corpselike, the clean white bedding defining his hill of a belly and planklike feet. Both eyes are closed but his mouth is slung open on one side, like a fish's mouth being dragged by a hook. Moving closer, she can see how the whole half of his face sags downwards, as if gravity is stronger on that side of the bed. Five days ago, while lawn bowling at the club, her uncle suffered a stroke, his entire right side paralyzed. How is it that the brain can split the body so cleanly down the middle?

Hands clasped at his chest, her uncle's wrists are hooked up to various needles and tubes. She slowly places both her hands over his. One side of his mouth lifts in a smile before an eyelid pops opens.

"Ecca." His tipped tongue mangles her name.

"Uncle Tony." She smiles, relieved to see his mind all there behind that eye. She smoothes the hair from his forehead.

"Ha ah —"

"Shh, I get to do the talking for a change."

Becca pulls a brand new Discman and tiny headset from her bag. "First, a gift from Aunt Maudie. And," she removes a small shoebox, "I've burned compilations of all your favourites."

He nods approvingly, an angled nod.

"How about if I massage your feet, which Aunt Maudie tells me you like, catch you up on my life, and then I'll leave you with Tony Bennett, or would you prefer Beethoven today?"

"Ozar."

"Mozart?"

He winks.

She tugs free a bed corner, lifts the sheet and, without looking, feels for a foot. The skin is hard and sandpapery, wiry hairs on top. She starts out tentative until he moans in pleasure, visibly relaxing under her hands.

"Well, in the world of tennis," she begins, "namely Wimbledon, which Noel says he's going to get us tickets for next year." Her uncle makes a gutteral sound, "ow," which she takes for wow and continues. "Federer lost to Nadal if you can believe it. It's the grass; Nadal could never beat him on clay." Her thumb hits what feels like a plantars wart or corn. "And Sarina lost to Henin-Ardenne, who's suddenly undeafeatable." Uncle Tony lifts his thumb. He never cared for Sarina and what he calls her "histrionics."

"Noel and I are going to make the most of what's left of the summer before school starts. Aunt Maudie says we can take out the boat." His good eyebrow rises. "Yes, we'll take the best of care and we'll oil it down after. Don't worry."

"We're planning to canoe up the Nashwack to that beach I've told you about. We're making an outrageous picnic." Her uncle groans long and loud. "You'll be eating solids soon enough." She can't find a toenail on his middle toe. "We'll save you some caviar."

Uncle Tony takes his good hand and points feebly to the ring finger of the other.

"No. No ring yet. We're getting there," she says. Last night replays in her brain. Noel finally got a cramp in his jaw and had to stop. "And you'll be the first to know, Uncle Tony, rest assured. Now let's have your other foot then," she says, before realizing it may have no feeling in it.

LEAVING THE HOSPITAL, Becca heads to Maria's, her favourite delicatessen, to buy for Saturday's picnic. Imagine, she thinks as she waits to be served, if she went to her grave never having had an orgasm. Never knowing what such a momentous human experience felt like. Terrible. It would be terrible. Maybe it's that something is lacking in her character. Something essential, like the ability to fully trust another person and therefore surrender oneself. And if so, did this really keep her from truly loving someone? Noel seemed to think so.

"Hi Maria. Some Gorgonzola, please."

Maria slices a wedge of Gorgonzola and wraps it in paper. "This cheese better than sex," she says in her thick Spanish tongue, then smiles slyly.

"I believe you," she says, taking the package. The man in line behind her snickers and she feels herself blush. Clearly she doesn't know what these people know.

All month she's put great effort into coming on her own. Years ago, she'd discovered boxes of soft-core paperbacks at the back of Aunt Maudie's bedroom closet. Stories full of tanned construction workers, muscled fireman, horny postmen, all wanting to provide uncomplicated great sex and unwilling to take a feeble no for an answer. She read a dozen of them, in bed working her arm into a charley horse, or propped under the spigot in the bath, the warm water battering her crotch numb. Lots of promising sensations but no gold ring. Mostly she felt self-conscious and worried about being heard through the thin walls of her apartment. In the end, Becca wondered if something wasn't broken down there.

She did note that none of her aunt's books described just how warped the woman looked and sounded as she roared up and over that edge. Can it be that easy for everyone but her?

THE DAY IS WEATHER PERFECT. Becca and Noel manoeuvre the canoe down from the car roof and carry it to the river's edge before transferring their picnic supplies. Caviar and champagne, roast duck and smoked salmon, homemade French loaf, Greek potato salad and marinated asparagus spears. For dessert, Maria's cheese with Danish pears. Noel has brought a tablecloth, candles and candle holder (even though it's daytime), all the necessary table settings, a foot pump and inflatable mattress. Dressed in the matching Tilley hats Noel had purchased, they push off, Noel steering in the back, Becca in front.

As soon as they get across the widest section of the river, Noel brings up the subject.

"Becca, I want you to tell me exactly what it is you're afraid of."

"Sorry?" She doesn't look around.

"In failing to reach orgasm, you've never said exactly what goes through that head of yours. I think we have to approach this problem from the other end, so to speak. You know I love you, so please, talk to me."

"Noel, first of all the words *failing* and *problem* are hardly helpful. Please don't make such a huge thing about it or I'll likely never get there." Her tone is curt, defensive, and for a long moment there is only the liquid sound of their paddles pushing away water.

"But," Becca takes a deep breath, "I think I'm afraid of losing control of myself."

"You won't turn inside out, you know."

"Well, I think I may surprise you with a very uncharacteristic display."

"Becca, I would be quite tickled to see you get, well, a little feral." Noel's voice has risen into his throat.

"But if I make unseemly noises and thrust my hips —"

"Sweetheart, stop, before I take you here in the canoe," he interrupts. "Maybe we should change the subject until we've arrived at our spot and had a glass of champagne. But I think, my love," his tone turns grand, "that this will be a day for the diary."

Becca suddenly remembers being nine years old at the dinner table, the revulsion on her father's face after a ringing burp escaped her lips. He started calling her "Rebecca" after that, "Princess" no longer applicable. It'll be all right, she tells herself. Times have changed. Still, she's going to ask Noel to wear the things she's brought along.

After entering the Nashwack tributary, they have to paddle hard against the undercurrent. She enjoys the effort. She loves this river with its peaceful beauty and hidden muscle braiding and unbraiding itself. Uncle Tony had introduced her to "St. John" as he called it. Taught her how to read its currents, its "moods," and planted wonder in Becca about what sorts of lives were lived beneath its surface. It was because of him she had chosen biology as her major.

Having worked up both a sweat and an appetite, they arrive at Cow Pie Island, one of several small uninhabited islands used for cattle grazing. The animals are ferried over from the mainland in the morning and collected up each evening.

As they drive the boat into shore, she sees the large weeping willow growing sideways out of the bank. Concealed under its drapery is where she and Noel first made love, one year ago today. And here they are, back again, armed with a mattress after Noel had scraped half the skin off his knees that first time.

They remove their boaters and step into the sun-warmed water. Sand sticks to their feet as they transport their things into the shaded shelter, swallows rustling from their hiding places and flying off. Lastly, they drag up the canoe, tuck it horizontally under the hang of the bank.

"Must hide the evidence," smiles Noel. "Hate to be caught with our skivvies down."

"I'm with you," Becca agrees, clearly apprehensive.

"Sweetie, come over here."

As they embrace, cows low in the distance. Time to get on the ferry, she thinks as Noel kisses the top of her forehead then the tip of her nose. "It's our anniversary, let's just enjoy ourselves."

She smiles up at him.

"And each other," he adds.

"Happy anniversary," she says, and they kiss on the mouth, tongues fencing playfully. Hers tires well before his and they end with a slurpy kiss.

"Okay, let's set up," he says, rubbing his hands together.

They tie back some of the willow branches to create a proper ceiling then spread a blanket between two rocks. Noel sets out the candlesticks and candles then opens one of the Tupperware bins and slips out a piece of duck.

"Just a little protein to keep my strength up," he says, eyebrows dancing. He offers the container to Becca. "Awful good."

"No, thanks. I'll wait." She's hungry, but too worried to eat yet.

Noel proceeds to fill the inflatable double mattress. It's a deep blue colour with fake velveteen on one side. Pumping his foot up and down on the accordion pump, Noel reminds her of a square dance caller. *Lick your partner round and round, make her squeal or lose her crown.*

"While I'm doing this, why don't you open up the champagne?" he suggests.

"I've never opened a bottle of champagne."

"First time for everything," he says and his eyes widen. "You can practice your groaning."

"Noel," she says, and he laughs his chipper laugh, staccato, like dolphin-speak.

She removes the foil paper and wire cage, then stabilizes the bottle between her thighs to get a grip on the cork.

"I don't," she tries to speak while straining, " know if I can —"

The cork releases with a minor explosion and a scream from Becca. Wine bubbles up over the sand.

"Quick," Noel instructs, "drink the overflow. Can't waste a fifty-dollar bottle of bubbles."

She puts her mouth over the bottle and gags on the fizz.

"See you did it, Becca." He holds up a teaching finger. "Surprised yourself. Now give me a glass of that stuff. Is it as dry and smooth as that fellow purported?"

"Lovely," Becca says, her head swooning from drinking on an empty stomach. She pours two glasses and they taste it together.

"Yes, not bad at all. Rakishly dry with a jasmine slide to it. I'm pleased."

Noel gives the mattress a press with his foot. "I'd say this thing is ready for a test run."

"Me too," she says, the champagne boosting her confidence. "But wait." She goes to her backpack. "I thought it would be a help if you wore a little something for me. I think it could make all the difference."

"Oh?"

She holds up a small circular plastic case. "Some earplugs." In her other hand is a pink satin eye mask trimmed in black lace. "And Aunt Maudie's night mask."

"Oh."

"I know it seems ridiculous but I think if you can't see or hear me, I'll be less inhibited. It's just to get me over the hump."

As he spreads his arms like a martyr, she can tell he's suppressing laughter. "I will don or remove whatever you desire, Becca my love, but you must do the honours of the dressing and undressing. And before we get started, a toast."

He retrieves the bottle from the picnic blanket and tops up both their glasses.

"To the unexpected."

"To the unexpected." She laughs nervously and they clink glasses. Noel downs his entire glass and she follows suit. As he removes their empty glasses to the picnic blanket, she breathes in the warm air, senses the river's push and pull and thinks how perfect this spot of earth.

"I am at your disposal," says Noel. He closes his eyes and lets his arms dangle by his sides.

"Not a word out of you then," she scolds before letting her voice swing low. "I'm going to be concentrating very hard."

Noel mimes zipping up his mouth. She places the cushioned mask over his tipped head and notices, for the first time, a patch of pink skin where his hair has thinned on top. She likes his hair and wonders how much he'll lose over time. She shapes one doughy earplug between her palms and glances down to sees an erection already straining his zipper. She feels a rush of horniness and gives his zipper a tap.

"You just hold your horses, fella," she says, and Noel giggles girlishly.

When his ears are plugged she tests him with a fairly loud, "Hey!" He doesn't flinch. Good enough, she thinks. If she yells, it'll at least be muffled.

She unbuttons Noel's shirt and softly encircles the hair around his nipples with her fingertips. He shivers and grabs up her arms to lower her down onto the plumped mattress. Blind and smiling, he feels around to undo her pants and then removes them along with her underwear. Then, after asking her to slide up on the mattress some, he raises his masked face, howls like a wolf, then dives between her thighs.

Keep breathing, she tells herself, rolling her head back and forth on the mattress. This is serious business. Moan, wiggle, make sounds. Let it happen, let it come. I'm ready, willing and able, she affirms. I do love and trust this man and he loves me. Let's go, here we go, up and over.

The internal dialogue scatters as bodily sensations take over. Her focus reduces to the area just under his tongue and a familiar tension begins its ascent. Her muscles engage one by one, wrapping up her legs, her buttocks, creeping up her torso, and pinching her head as if to a point. Her body a quivering needle wanting to puncture something, blast off, be split apart like kindling. Man-up, Becca tells herself, we are going to go for it. She takes a deep breath. Now.

She can feels the surprise in Noel's hands as his grip tightens on her hips to keep contact with his tongue. She grabs fistfuls of his hair, needing something to hang onto. He makes a squeaking sound that she simply ignores. She's determined, goddamnit, and just hopes she doesn't hurt him. Displaced air repeatedly bucks the mattress and Noel coughs but doesn't stop what he's doing. She manoeuvres her legs under his shoulders, locks her ankles behind his back. She's being physically generous to herself for the first time. She's just going to take what she needs without asking permission. Noel's presence begins to blur.

Minutes later, she's tossing her head and moaning, clenching Noel between her thighs. Pleasurable sensations rush round her nerves but still don't go anywhere new. She moans louder. Nothing. What is wrong with me? Worried Noel might be suffering down there, she lifts up her head to check on him.

Her aunt's mask is lifted on one side and Noel has one wide, panicky eye turned towards the picnic things. Becca glances over and sees a raccoon nibbling voraciously on a piece of duck he's holding in his claws. She laughs out loud at this anniversary folly of theirs, and suddenly that laugh becomes part howl, part scream. Her body has turned to frozen fire. She can no longer see the summit – she is the summit.

BECCA COVERS HER FACE and collapses in a fit of laughter that flirts with tears. A skunklike scent is rising from her armpits and sweat from her brow is running into one eye. Wow...wow...wow. When her laughter finally peters out, she dares spread her fingers and peek up at Noel. He's kneeling, removing mask and earplugs.

"Oh my gosh," she says, wiping the sweat from her eyes. "Noel, that was incredible."

"Well done, darling." He removes the earplugs and looks over at the picnic things. "You scared off a horde of raccoons and surprised the punch right out of me."

She hears the dryness in his voice. He stands. His erection is gone. "I could use more of that champagne about now." He starts to button up his shirt. "Terribly thirsty."

He fills his glass only, takes a long drink, then begins scouting around, mumbling about the raccoon thieving their duck and "what a waste on such a palate. My own fault, of course, for not securing the lid."

Alone on the mattress, Becca stares up at the nodding branches of the willow. She wants to have sex, in some fantastic position, wants to come again and knows she can, but everything has changed.

"We really should eat up, my love, before the heat gets the best of everything."

"There's cheese," she says, more to herself.

Noel's back is turned as she retrieves her pants and underwear. She takes her time, tucks in her shirt, finger combs her hair. As Noel fusses over setting out the food, she ducks outside the umbrella of their tree and, without a word, walks down to the water's edge. He neither calls after her nor follows. The sun is dropping behind the trees and the water is a hushed gunmetal grey. A crow shrieks from somewhere on the far shore. Becca squats and dips her hands in the water causing a school of tadpoles to burst apart like fireworks.

Puck

THE HOUSE LIGHTS DIM AND THE HEAVY curtain lifts to a near-empty stage. Martin's stomach involuntarily clenches. Upstage right stands one lone tree made from a clunky black frame filled in with gray gauze. This singular drab piece of scenery is set against a black backdrop which is dissected in half by a white scrim. It looks as if the scrim has become stuck during its lowering. A teenage boy from the company's school, a boy known for talking too much in class, walks across the stage as plainly as if walking across the street, and stands facing the audience. He is dressed in a sheetlike toga and wears, on his head, a sparkly silver turban that resembles soft ice cream. "His poo poo do," was how the designer, Vaughn, described it.

The boy clears his throat and unrolls a piece of parchment. He presents the premise of the ballet's first act, reading a little too fast in dumbed-down

Shakespearean. Then the boy walks offstage as gracelessly as he walked on. He has done exactly what he's been instructed by Martin to do. The music begins and Vaughn, sitting beside Martin, gleefully pinches Martin's thigh.

THE BOARDROOM LIGHTS hung low over the table, leaving members' faces in half shadow; Martin appreciated the slightly Gothic effect. He watched the board's president pore over the minutes, lips moving, pushing the words along, and imagined the man's curly blond head morphing into a sheep's, a pale stubby tongue, the same nervous, bleating eyes. Martin turned his chair to face the window, the June sky. The sun was a bloated blood orange, the torn clouds a heated pink bordering on fuchsia. Now those should be the colours for Andrea's fire costume, he mused, not your typical reds and yellows. Throw in some copper, a cerulean blue. He pictured Vaughn's drawing: Andrea in corset bodice, a drop-waisted skirt of stiff layers of taffeta and netting, hair wired to stream behind her, the ends on fire. They hadn't quite figured out the fire bit yet. How he loved Andrea in costume. Costumes transformed her from ordinary human into high art. He ran a hand over his buzzed head, enjoying the feel of the soft nap going against the grain.

Below in the street, Mrs. Morley, late for the meeting, came around the corner, head down, pitching side to side. He could tell she was hurrying the best her body allowed. Since she was the secretary, the meeting couldn't begin without her. A long square navy shirt and ankle-length skirt effectively obliterated any physical definition. She was a roving mass of material with head and feet. He wondered how it felt to live in such an obese body. Had her nerves gone numb under all those layers, or did she somehow disassociate from her flesh? She was a recent addition to the board and he knew nothing about her except that she taught Art History up at the university. As a professor, she probably lived more in her mind than her flesh, he thought. A mind, after all, weighed nothing at all.

PUCK POKES HIS HEAD OUT from behind the tree to the sound of a synthesized cricket and synthesized water tumbling over rocks. His hair is bleached white and spiked up in rows crossing his head like the crown on the Statue of Liberty. There is one larger spike over his forehead like a diminutive unicorn horn. Puck leaps in "puckish" *pas-de-chats* across the floor before making a swivelling turn and finishing with his back to the audience. There in full view are his flexed buttocks, barely veiled in sheer grey tights over a more or less invisible thong. Whispers ripple through the house. Shock, appreciation, or dismay? wonders Martin, wincing at the costume's three white rattails of hair that extend from Puck's head and are sewn down the back of the unitard. Each skinny braid varies in length, the longest one trailing off one bum cheek like an off-centre tail. Ugly.

"We'll call it postmodern neostructuralist homo-fascist," Vaughn had said in the planning stages. "I'll go minimalist and dress everyone in thongs. Husbands will be bringing their wives back to see it two or three times."

Martin had commissioned James Stokes – an old friend – for the score. Jimmy had a drinking problem, was always strapped for cash, and hadn't had a commission for years. He took the job at half of what it would have cost hiring any other composer. The music, entirely synthesized, was atonal and arrhythmic. "The score's subtle and a challenge," Martin had told the dancers after the initial confusion and complaints, "but I know you're up to it." He'd suggested they move *through* the sounds and hated himself for it.

Fat Mrs. Morley is sitting in the row just in front of him – the board members' row. He notices that her attention has drifted into the aisle.

THE MINUTES finally approved, the president, Glenn Levine, read out the first agenda item. "Winter and spring season repertoire."

Winifred (Winnie) Bower, head of fundraising – mainly because of her husband's fathomless pockets – raised her arm at a perfect right angle. Her long black hair undulated back from her forehead and was caught under a wide silver headband, which matched her silver bracelet of similar width and a tubular silver necklace. Her armour, thought Martin, imagining a corset under her silk blouse of the same solid silver, a chastity belt whose key has cost her husband hundreds of thousands over the years. Winnie squared her *haute couture* shoulders with a repulsive little shimmy and Martin had to look away. Not looking at her face would help him bear what came out of her mouth.

"We all know what a success *The Lovers* was last season. Which, as everyone knows, put us back in the black." She clapped and a few others followed suit.

Martin scanned the company photos along the wall, landing on one of Andrea in Don Q. The aesthetic of her arabesque line made his blood surge. He could just barely make out the peanut-shaped birthmark on her exposed ribcage. Where she was kissed by genius was what he told her whenever he kissed it himself.

"I have no doubt Martin's ballet will be performed for decades to come, and not just by our company. So I am proposing to our talented artistic director," Winnie paused and Martin could feel her tight, weasel-like smile pulling on him, "that he choreograph a second Shakespearean-based work for this year's winter offering."

What? Martin tried to not let his shock show on his face. Glenn had promised he could mount *Human Elements* this winter. Why in hell hadn't he got something in writing?

Glenn nervously cleared his throat. "Well, that's one proposal on the table. Thank you, Winnie. Now, I do believe Martin was hoping to do an abstract work? With a nature theme? Maybe Martin could explain his idea to us?" His head jutted forward on his neck as if offering itself to be butchered. His sheep head, thought Martin, and imagined cutting out the tongue.

PUCK CALLS HIS FELLOW FAERIES out of the wood-less woods and a half dozen men and women skip and cartwheel onto the stage. This entrance is totally improvised and Martin squints in order only to half see. All the faeries are dressed in the same thong and transparent bodysuit. The audience seems to lean forward collectively in their seats, for a better look.

Martin had brought in two retired dancers to play the old faerie king and queen. Mr. Bruckner had done numerous character roles since his retirement, but Miss Parsons, whose dancer's shape had long expired, was as surprised by Martin's request as she was grateful. Pocketing the chubby queen, a white walnut shell sways and creaks as it descends from the fly system. It looks dangerous. Below, the dancers face upstage in a welcoming V-shape, creating two stag-gered rows of beautiful bums.

Vaughn leans over and whispers, "Their favourite butt is all they'll remember."

MARTIN LEANED BACK in his chair, crossed his arms and focused on the plate of sugared Timbits centred on the boardroom table. He disliked trying to sell himself and his ideas, knew he wasn't personable enough to be any good at it. They hired him to be the artist and should leave these decisions to him.

"Titled *Human Elements*, the evening would explore the five elements versus man." Martin tucked in his chin and elongated his dancer's neck. As much as he wished he was smiling, making eye contact and putting lively expression behind his words, something in him refused. He would not, could not, ingratiate himself. "Internally, each element will relate to an emotion: the winds of aggression, the fires of craving, the mulishness of earth, the watery depth of despair, the metallic shine of arrogance. Riding the energy of emotion, the dancers will transmute from humans into elemental forces and back again."

He glanced once around the table. Nobody was looking at him except Mrs. Morley across from him. Her pen hand had stopped moving and a half-eaten doughnut hole was suspended in front of her mouth. Her dark gray hair was cut at straight Cleopatra angles, a fashionable scarf around her neck helping to hide the folds of her chin. Magnified behind her glasses, her large dark eyes looked rapt. Encouraged, he refocused on the Timbits and continued.

"The score, a striking piece by Frederick Lieberson, will incorporate elemental sounds – running water, rushing wind, that kind of thing – as well as human voice. Contralto, I'm asking for." Martin took a breath. "And the questions posited: Are man and nature comprised of the same destructive and creative forces? What is the quality of the experience when these internal and external forces become one?"

These were questions Martin had no answers for. He believed uncertainty fostered creativity and would decide on answers only after the choreography had revealed itself. Again Martin glanced around the table. With the exception of Mrs. Morley, who wore a small, animated smile, nobody seemed to have the faintest idea what he was talking about.

"Your," Winnie washed the air with a hand, "windy piece, Martin, sounds very intriguing, but I have to say that the majority of our audience finds the abstract stuff very difficult to follow."

Martin knew she was referring to *Checklist*, a ballet he mounted two years ago about society's obsession with getting things done, the faster the better. With the exception of Montreal, where it played to full houses, it completely bombed at the box office.

"Call them unsophisticated, but we do have to keep our audience in mind." She tipped her head at a condescending angle implying him naïve, of knowing pathetically little about the business side of things. He didn't know how to defend himself against the obvious. He was naïve about the business side; he chose to be so.

"Besides," continued Winnie, her face lighting up, "who doesn't like listening to a story when it's cold and dark outside?"

"Listening?" said the treasurer, Patty Lamb. Her voice sounded anxious, sounded rehearsed.

"Well, I was thinking maybe we could have a narrator, dressed in period costume, reading from the original play," said Winnie, glassy eyed and weirdly staring, as if attempting to hypnotize her listeners.

Board members shifted uncomfortably in their seats.

"I will gladly adapt a second Shakespeare play for the following season, but I've done quite a lot of work on *Human Elements*, as has our designer —"

"I honestly don't think I can raise the necessary money for this year, Martin," said Winnie flatly. She shook her head sadly yet firmly.

Martin disliked confrontation, avoided it whenever possible. And he believed artists shouldn't have to defend themselves, much less their work.

"If you put your elemental piece off for a year," she continued, "and give people something they don't have to work too hard for, win people's confidence for another season, then they'll be more willing to follow where you lead." She sighed. "I'm sorry, Martin, really I am, but I believe it's too soon."

Winnie pushed her starry gaze around the table and other heads began to murmur in agreement.

"I think Martin's ballet sounds very exciting," said Mrs. Morley. "And considering the state of the world, it seems timely and rather appropriate really."

Martin tried to recall if he'd ever heard the secretary addressed by her first name. It's something beautiful, he thought, like Isabelle or Olivia.

The secretary continued. "It put me in mind of the ancient Greek mytho —"

"You're absolutely right," said Winnie, cutting her off. She leaned towards Mrs. Morley and enunciated slowly and clearly, "It's just that is it too soon for our patrons."

"Perhaps I can put off *Elements* until the following year," murmured Martin.

"Are you sure?" bleated Glenn, sounding greatly relieved.

"I'm sure, if we write it into the contract," said Martin, and Glenn quickly indicated to Mrs. Morley to make a note of that.

Winnie quietly studied her bracelet, down playing her victory.

"Okay then," said Glenn throwing up his hooves. "Shall we have a vote?"

"Martin, I had one more little thought about the new ballet, if you don't mind?" said Winnie. "I was thinking *A Midsummer Night's Dream*. Wouldn't that be fun for winter? I know you artists love contrast."

HAVING PUSHED BACK THE FURNITURE and rolled back the rug, Andrea marked out her solo in front of the living room's floor to ceiling windows. She wanted to make sure she remembered it before heading into the studio. She glanced at the street one floor below. Though the sun was shining, she could tell it was cold out by the way scarves covered mouths and toques were pulled low over ears. Look up here, she thought. She hated practicing if no one was watching. Her solo was surprisingly simple really, more like a classroom exercise, with lots of stops and poses. The simplicity was probably significant to the overall theme, she guessed, or to her character's, Hermia's, youth and determination.

"I will not marry Demetrius no matter what Uncle threatens," she stated before a *chaisse* into a whirlwind

of *chainne* turns that deposited her in the middle of a
window. She punctuated her finish by crossing her
arms in front of her chest and pouting. These character gestures were her idea. Oddly enough, Martin, the
control freak, had told the dancers they were welcome
to improvise here and there. At first they had assumed
he was being sarcastic. But he wasn't. He actually said
he was trying a new approach to help marry the indi-
vidual with his or her character. For the first time,
thought Andrea, as she lunged into a circular *porte de
bras*, knocking her elbow into the couch, Martin was
giving people credit for having some creative talent of
their own. It was about time, really. Roman, though
only a corps dancer, was especially talented. She'd seen
a video of this amazing piece he did for his sister's
company in Halifax. Had promised him she'd show
Martin when the time seemed right.

Reverse *sutenu, passé*, fourth and *pirouette*. Martin
was in such a shitty mood lately and didn't want to
talk about anything studio related. For his other bal-
lets, he'd used her as a sounding board, asked her
opinions on a piece, her sense of how the dancers
were responding.

"Because the music's so impossible to count, the
dancers are finding they have to be super cued into
each other," she offered last night at dinner. "They've
developed little visual codes for timing." He wasn't
interested. She told him how Shauna, the ballet master, had referred to his ensemble choreography as
"neoclassical purity." He'd rolled his eyes. He had
never thought much of Shauna's opinion.

She marked out her combination as it travelled upstage into the dining room. Nothing she did, at home or in the studio, cheered him up. Even in their lovemaking, he seemed distracted. Maybe their age difference was starting to show. And now the *jeté, tour jeté* combination. She travelled around the coffee table and back to the window. Or maybe he was moving on and couldn't tell her. He'd never confront her. He'd leave it to her to end things. Anything to avoid a scene.

A courier van pulled up in front of their apartment building. Probably the final changes to the score. She hoped it was the same guy who made last week's delivery. She waited until he stepped from the van. Even though he was wearing a toque and sunglasses, she could tell it was him. She immediately resumed dancing, stepped closer to the window exaggerating her movements. Package and clipboard in hand, he started towards the steps, stopped and looked up. Yes, smiled Andrea as she unfurled her willowy arms then tossed a foot behind to touch the back of her head. She finished off with a triple *pirouette*, her knee just barely missing the window frame. Landing the turn, she assumed a pensive nonchalance then walked away from the window.

A few seconds later, the intercom buzzed.

"Yes?" She dragged the elastic from her ponytail.

"Courier."

She rang him in. When she heard his footsteps on the stairs, she dropped her head forward, her hair sweeping the floor, then whipped it back to fan out across her shoulders. Black dance pants hung low on her hips not quite meeting her blue T-shirt, her taut belly slightly exposed. He knocked, she counted to five then slowly unbolted the door and opened it.

"Package for Kenyon?" He'd removed his hat and was as cute as she'd remembered.

She didn't answer, just gave an almost imperceptible nod, a contained smile. She wanted him to work for it, could feel him studying her through the green lenses of his sunglasses. He slipped a pen from his shirt pocket and scribbled his initials next to Martin's name. His shirt was clean but unironed. His arm was nicely muscled.

"You must be a dancer?" he said and slid the glasses to the top of his head. A blond arrow of hair fell over one blue eye. He didn't remove it, which left him partially masked. Nice. He knew how to work it too, she thought.

"Why?" she asked.

"I saw you practicing in the window."

"Oh, that's embarrassing."

"Looked amazing to me."

"Do I have to sign something?" She swallowed a smile and ran a hand through her hair.

"Yeah, right here by the *x*."

She took his pen and their knuckles brushed, his cold to the touch. Neither of them hurried to remove their hands.

"Do you, like, have any shows coming up?" He shrugged with a shy kind of confidence. Too sexy.

She handed back the pen and clipboard and he handed over the manila envelope.

"You like the ballet?" Hugging the envelope to her chest, she leaned against the door jamb.

"Uh, never really been but would go to see you."

She held his eye for a second longer than she should.

"I'm performing in three weeks. The show's based on Shakespeare's *Midsummer Night's Dream*."

"Cool. I actually read that. Well, back in high school."

"I get a couple of comps. I could leave one for you at the box office, say, for opening night? That's a Thursday."

"That would be great."

"Um. I'll need your name."

"Paul. Paul Simard." He extended his hand. He didn't shake her hand as much as felt how it fit in his. "And yours?"

"Andrea Roth."

"Andrea," he repeated.

"When you come, send me a note backstage with your seat number," she said, trying to sound offhand.

"Why?" he asked with a curious smile that dimpled his left cheek. Adorable.

"I just like to be able to pick out people I know in the audience. It entertains me," she said softly, embarrassed now.

What she didn't say is that she always picked out a face to dance to, usually Martin if he was watching, and dedicated every muscle to his tortuous seduction.

"So, see you onstage," he said, flashing another dimpled smile. He slowly, playfully, lowered his sunglasses back onto his nose and Andrea lost her cool and laughed.

"Maybe I could take you out after?" he asked.

She didn't answer, just held his eye and slowly shut the door, her nerves stinging.

THE GIANT SHELL lands with a bump and the Faerie Queen frowns with mock displeasure. The audience responds with a smattering of uncertain laughter. The queen flutters a hand to summon her flock of teenaged slave boys, costumed in their toga sheets and poo poo turbans. She proceeds to toy with an exposed nipple of the nearest boy and more tentative amusement trickles through the audience. As if unable to hold back any longer, one person down front hoots with laughter.

The queen snaps her ringed fingers and a second group of teenaged boys enters. Each carries a plate of food. Real food. She bats her fake eyelashes, rubs her hands together and proceeds to eat. Vaughn had thought watching a person eating real food on stage instead of pantomiming with plastic would be so alien to an audience of ballet-goers as to be shocking. Picking up a creamed horn, the queen sticks out her tongue and slowly pokes it into the round end of the pastry. Winnie snickers, then turns to give Martin an eyebrow raised *you-rascal-you* look. Martin shivers.

The Faerie King makes his melodramatic entrance dressed in an absurdly phallic Medusa-like headdress. Two lesser faeries hold his twelve-foot-long forest green cape at each end and billow it up and down behind him, parachute style. The cape is removed with a cartoon flourish and the seasoned king stands baring his flaccid backside. "Ughs" erupt from the front rows. Vaughn has to hold a hand over his mouth he's laughing so hard.

When it becomes obvious that the king prefers the slave boys to his wife there is more bawdy laughter. In cahoots with gay young Puck, the king schemes to have his way with the queen's boys.

PACING THE GREEN ROOM, Martin jumped as a finger jabbed his ribs.

"Nervous, are we?" Vaughn lowered his voice. "Tonight's a toss off, Martin. A joke. Don't start taking yourself seriously now." He patted Martin's shoulder. Vaughn wore black leather pants and black silk shirt with brown leather tie. On his feet were his dusty-looking brown suede cowboy boots, which he called his "Brokeback" boots. A series of black hoops lined one ear and his dark hair was slicked straight back to reveal a kind of inverted widow's peak. He looked elegantly sinister.

Though Martin usually wore a good suit for opening night, he'd dressed down in black jeans and sports coat, his shirt open at the collar. He didn't feel worthy of a tie.

"I can hardly believe my name is on that program. Maybe if we'd labelled it "experimental theatre" instead of "world premiere."

"Humility is good for the artistic soul. So, do you think they'll get the title. That the queen is actually the king?" Vaughn guided him to the door leading to the house. "Come on. Let's go sit down. And don't look so worried. I'll direct the clapping." He began whistling "Springtime for Hitler in Germany".

"Stop it," said Martin.

Martin had granted a brief interview earlier in the week to the dance critic for *The Post*. "It's an exploration of relationships," he'd told her, "their often questionable moorings and the inevitable changes that arise as people grow and their needs change. We have updated Shakespeare with themes of obsessive compulsion and sexual reorientation. The bleakness of the sets and costumes is to contrast the nature of passion and its colourful consequences."

He told the critic, and it was true, that he had relinquished a healthy amount of choreographic responsibility to the dancers. "All things considered," Martin concluded, "it's a very *avant-garde* piece." He hated the word *avant-garde*, thought it reeked of the worst sort of pretension. A brain tumour, is what he had wanted to say. They'd found a brain tumour on his cerebral cortex, which was affecting his ability to discriminate.

Martin made his way down the aisle behind Vaughn, heads turning his way in recognition. He kept his eyes to himself and they found their seat in the reserved section in centre-orchestra. As on every opening night, the board members occupied the row in front of them.

"Check out Winifred's tiara," whispered Vaughn.

Winnie Bower sat between her doughnut-haired husband and Patty Lamb. She was wearing a jewel-studded headband, flapper style, that picked up the house lights and glittered whenever she moved.

"Do you think those jewels are real?" continued Vaughn.

Martin noticed Mrs. Morley sitting alone at the end of the aisle, filling her seat like risen dough over-flowing its bowl. Her stillness was almost regal, her moon of a face shining in anticipation toward the stage, a stunning olive and beige scarf wrapping her neck. There was an empty seat between her and Glenn Levin's English-challenged boyfriend, Diego. Since each board member received two comps, he imagined her husband recently passed away or her best friend hospitalized. He felt for her before it occurred to him that she simply didn't want someone beside her, making comments and distracting her from the stage. It was the way *he* preferred watching performances, given the choice. Maybe, unlike all these pretenders, this fat woman was a true ballet afi-cionado. In that case, he did feel for her. And was ashamed for himself. He would have been far less miserable these past months if he'd dropped his resentment over the board's decision and simply com-mitted himself to this damn ballet. If he had done this ballet in earnest, Martin wanted to tell her, Puck and the other faeries would have tall swallowtail wings attached shoulder to calf and made of pale green silk painted with eyelike circles that pulsed colour. The set would breathe with the first greens of spring: a backdrop of sensual forest stroked in light, lush vines overhead tipped in gold, gobos of leaves shimmering over the floor.

AS SOON AS ANDREA, as Hermia, steps onstage, Martin can see she's exceptionally focused, absolutely on point. She portrays her character with surprising spine which, together with a kind of pouty sexiness, is very becoming. She knows that he's in the audience yet is playing to the left side of the house for some reason. He silently admonishes her to look in his direction.

Vaughn had costumed the human characters drably: the women in plain white dresses and bare legs, the men in white pants and short-sleeved shirts that lay open at the neck to display the male clavicle – Vaughn's favourite body part. The more serious drama of the humans works surprisingly well against the slapstick faeries, thinks Martin. Who would have thought? His choreography, though, is as soulless as the so-called music. But what bothers him most is how these young men and women are committing themselves to the steps. Manoeuvring through this minefield of music, their dancing is earnest and flawless. He's used them and deceived them and still they are working their exposed butts off. Andrea, as Hermia, is somehow infusing his simplistic steps with emotional depth. She is even able to counterpoint the monochrome music in a way that brings out an intricacy of sound he didn't believe Jimmy capable of anymore.

As act one nears its end, the music shifts to the inane knocking of glockenspiels. Mrs. Morley discreetly plugs one ear with her finger.

"Jimmy must have been into the schnapps that night," whispers Vaughn.

Puck places a donkey's head on a drugged and sleeping Bottom, then leaps onto his back in a position suggestive of both bestiality and necrophilia. Martin can hardly believe he had taken this suggestion of Vaughn's and actually encouraged it in rehearsal. Addressing the audience, Puck places a finger to his lips and people erupt in laughter. The players freeze and the turbaned narrator saunters on and recaps the obvious. As the curtain comes down, the audience claps long and loud without Vaughn's assistance. Mrs. Morley, notices Martin, is not in her seat.

"This town is more lively than I thought," says Vaughn. "And didn't Clarisse do a realistic job on that ass head?"

The clapping dissipates as the house lights rise. Winnie leans over her seat and into Martin's face.

"You are quite the character, Martin," she announces so the people around them can hear. "I always thought of your work as so serious, but this is very funny and very daring."

Martin smiles weakly but Vaughn pipes right up. "That's the artist's job, Winnie. To keep you guessing."

"Join us in the lobby for a glass of wine?" offers Winnie.

"No, no," Martin says quickly. "I have things to check on backstage."

"I could use a glass," smiles Vaughn. "My throat is positively parched from all that hilarity."

AVOIDING FACES because he's afraid of what they might say, Martin makes his way to the green room.

"Hey, Martin." Roman, a robe covering his revealing costume, is there dropping coins into the Coke machine. "How did you like my *saute basque* combination on the faerie entrance, with the switch kick?"

"Yeah, good stuff," says Martin, though he'd squinted at that point and missed it.

"Would you mind if I changed it up, say, tomorrow night? I have another idea, something I don't think's been done before."

"No, uh, feel free."

"Thanks. Thanks a lot." Roman sounds sincerely grateful.

Oh, god, he needs air. Martin slips out a side door, cold air rushing into his lungs. Could people really not know the difference? Was it some sort of herd mentality? Group dementia? From his pocket, he fishes out a cigarette and his gold lighter.

Laughter travels from under the marquee where patrons, sipping wine, are, no doubt, lighting up like him. He draws smoke deep into his lungs, watches a young man with a lock of hair hanging over one eye trot by cradling flowers, red roses, one white one in their centre. Under the filmy light of the street lamp, the flowers look thick as velvet. A romantic, thinks Martin with a stab of envy and realizes that, in all his worry about tonight, he'd forgotten to buy Andrea her bouquet. They have an opening night ritual of exchanging gifts. He gives her the traditional bouquet, a mix that he carefully picks out himself, along with a card saying in a poetic way what each flower or colour represents. She comes up with something different each time: Belgian chocolates, an interesting tie, an expensive bottle of wine. Tonight on his desk was a small wooden dresser doll, hinged at the joints so it could be manipulated into various positions. She had bent the legs into a kneeling position, placed the wood block hands in prayer with the head bent forward. *Thanks for the dance*, read the card.

The young man knocks on the stage door and Martin wonders which of his dancers is the lucky recipient. Someone is obviously anticipating the young man's arrival because the door opens immediately.

It's Andrea, still in costume, her long hair fanned over her shoulders. Martin takes a quick step back into shadow and watches as his lover beams up at the young man before taking the roses and burying her nose in them the way she always does when Martin gives her flowers. Then, like she also always does, she gives the guy a kiss. On the lips. The parting slow and savoured. She pulls him inside and the door slowly closes behind them.

"Fuck," he sighs, looking up at the sky. Though it's a clear night, the city lights obliterate all but the brightest of stars. His mind has gone oddly blank, has thrown up a huge dam to keep a deluge of thoughts, of regrets, at bay.

The house lights begin to flicker behind him, calling people to take their seats. Martin draws hard on his cigarette, his lungs burning hotly.

Someone else is coming down the sidewalk. Pitching side to side, it's Mrs. Morley, coat on, purse slung over one padded shoulder, her striking scarf now a shawl banking her shoulders. She's leaving this night behind, he thinks, as the house lights blink on and off again. He watches her pass then drops his cigarette on the cement and catches up with her.

"Mrs. Morley," he says. "Mind if I walk with you?"

"Well, no, Martin, I don't mind at all." She looks surprised yet also not.

"I'm sorry, I don't know your first name."

"It's Audrey."

"Audrey," he repeats. "That's a lovely name."

MARTIN CALLED VAUGHN and told him the result of the board meeting.

"*Midsummer's Night's Dream*?" yelled Vaughn into the phone. "Don't they know it's been done to death. Fuck 'em, that's what I say. From that mealy-mouthed Glenn on down," said Vaughn. "You know, Martin, if *Lovers* hadn't been so successful, they wouldn't be trying to repeat themselves."

Martin had worked hard on *Lovers*, had dug deep to find an angle that inspired him, to give *Romeo and*

Juliet, the most overperformed story of all time, some fresh life.

"You know what I'm thinking?" continued Vaughn.

"What are you thinking, my fiendish friend."

"We sabotage the shit out of it."

Martin laughed. "I have to wonder if anyone would know the difference."

Vaughn paused, his tone turning thoughtful. "How's about a gay angle. Call it *Midsummer Night's Queens* for both the king and the queen. And really, I do love the name Puck."

Next

"BONJOUR AND WELCOME TO NEXUS CANADA telecommunication systems. For service in English, press one. Pour le service en Français —"

Standing in her spanking clean kitchen, Peggy presses number one for shut up. Her less than clean hair falls over her eye and she tucks it behind an ear. She swears half of it's fallen out since the baby.

"Welcome and thank you for choosing Nexus Canada, the fastest growing telecommunications company in North America." Where do they find these women with the unshakeable voices? Like mayonnaise in your ear. Nudging the cookie jar lid aside, Peggy slips out another Fudgeo. And why not a man's voice? Why are women's voices used for instilling patience, and men's for the exciting stuff like game show give-aways? She can't remember ever hearing a woman's voice bellow, "You've just won a brand new car!"

"All our service associates are currently serving other customers but your call is important to us –"

Associates. Give me air.

She tries to picture a human behind this voice and can't. An entire roomful of life-sized mechanized dolls is what she sees. Dolls with curvy red smiles, short dresses and big rubber boobs. Programmed for brain-dead, phones are attached to their robotic arms, which lift and lower on command. A short balding supervisor struts up and down the aisles making subtle adjustments to phone arms and cleavage. She turns the phone around to distance the annoying voice, pinching it between cheek and shoulder. If she stops responding to the commands, she knows she'll be forwarded to an operator that much quicker.

The cookie in her hand smells like bliss. She unscrews the halves, scrapes fudge filling onto her bottom teeth, stirs it with her tongue till it dissolves. Oh, yeah. She eats the less desirable wafers faithfully and with remorse, thinking they're slightly stale and that she might complain to the company.

Musak comes through the receiver now, the bouncy rhythm reminding her of Billy the Big Mouthed Bass. A week ago Sunday was her birthday. Duncan gave her an Anne Geddes calendar, a renewal of her *Canadian Living* magazine, a duster made from ostrich feathers and Billy. Her in-laws gave her an umbrella stroller for the baby – she thought it was her birthday – and another ceramic animal for the fake mantel over the fake fireplace. Her mother-in-law is a firm believer in figurines. Calls them "collectors' items" as if they'll be the first thing into a burglar's sack. *Get the animals*. All week, Peggy has been tempted to take her new ostrich duster and sweep the shitload of them into thin air, imagines tiny explosions as they hit the floor, animal heads rolling. This vision has become so satisfyingly real, she almost doesn't mind amassing more wide-eyed fawns struggling to stand on broken-looking legs. Oops. Smash.

Everyone else thought Duncan's gag fish was a laugh riot. When you pressed its red button, the mounted rubber bass thumped its tail to the music then lifted its head off the plaque to face you, flap its lips and sing a skewed version of "Take Me to the River." In a man's voice. The fish lips weren't synchronized to the song which, for some reason, infuriated her. Four-month-old Scotty cried whenever Duncan held him up to the singing fish head, which gave Duncan's mother an even bigger kick. A white-trash gift, Peggy thought at the time but kept her disappointment to herself.

Duncan insisted on hanging it on the stairwell wall in the middle of the Georgia O'Keefe cards she had framed. Duncan calls these her "snatch flowers," but Peggy knows they're real art because they're by a famous artist. Now Duncan presses Billy Bass's red button every time he comes upstairs. "I want to know, can you take me, I know the wayyy," followed by a thump, thump, thump of the tail, Duncan laughing his way to the bedroom. Genuine laughter.

"Thank you for holding, we do appreciate your patience."

"Patience," she sneers and turns the phone back around as if this might hurry things along.

Popping a mug of water in the microwave, she perches on a kitchen stool to wait, to hold. She's getting good at holding. Her whole life feels on fuckin hold. Out of the bottom of her pajama pants, her puffed ankles are covered with thorny black hairs that look plain ugly against her sun-starved skin. The swelling during the end of her pregnancy is not going away and her feet have magically outgrown all her old shoes except for her slippers. The pajamas are Duncan's, hers too tight around her waist right now. On days she doesn't walk down to the mall, she'll stay in pajamas until Duncan arrives home for supper. No point in getting dressed for herself. She and Scotty, pajama people. Like hospital folk.

She steeps the tea bag in the steaming water, adds milk, a spoon of honey. She misses her coffee buzz but decided, when pregnant, to switch to tea because it felt more civilized, less addictive. Lifting the cup to her mouth, she extends her pinky finger the way she's seen (or maybe just imagined) the Queen drink her tea, and senses the grace of a softened grip.

She takes tea and phone into the living room, listens for the baby monitor, which sits on top of the TV. Scotty is down for the first of two power naps. And judging from the monitor's utter quiet, he's sleeping like the dead. Must be his cold. She failed to bundle him enough on their walks or didn't wash her hands well enough before putting in his soother. Or didn't wash his soother well enough. But then maybe it's her milk. If she ate better – fewer cookies, more fruit...

"Your call is important to us and will be answered in the order in..."

Out the picture window, a dismal February sky contrasts their bright green lawn. A light drizzle makes the grass almost sparkle. Having grown up in New Brunswick, she finds the lawns here on the west coast – green in winter and brown in the summer – totally ass-backwards. After four years, she's still not used to it. She squints down at the garden.

"Shit, I mean shoot, look at that!" No cursing out loud, she reminds herself. She's a mother now, an example, a teacher even. But little green shoots with tiny purple heads are poking out of the soil! She planted all kinds of shit last fall after they moved in. She also planted the spikes with each plant's name and care instructions. She'll have to check later and see what the purple things are called. Pregnant as a barrel, she had dug a bed along either side of the front stoop the entire width of the house, and another one along the driveway. Duncan was afraid her digging like that was going to induce labour, yet he didn't offer to help. Two whole Safeway paycheques went to buying flowering bushes, flowering ground cover, and an assortment of bulbs to bloom in sequence. Or so the lady said. She and Duncan were just renting but the neighbours didn't need to know. Some day she would own a house, maybe even win one.

Theirs was a small box of a house in sore need of a paint job, but it was detached, which was what mattered.

Her child, she'd told Duncan, was not going to be raised in an apartment, unable to jump or yell for fear of upsetting the neighbours. Wasn't going to be listening to other people's televisions and other people's stupid pain and have them listening to yours. Duncan had been hot on renting a duplex near the garage where he worked, but she'd put her foot down.

She places the twice used tea bag in the compost bucket under the kitchen sink and gives her spoon a quick wash and dry before putting it back in its drawer. Keeping the house as clean as possible gives her a momentary sense of accomplishment. Yesterday there seemed no place left to clean until she thought to look up and saw graveyards of moths amassed in the bottoms of the light fixtures. Today, after researching a new phone company on the market, she's changing their long distance, Internet and email provider again. She'd registered online yesterday but something didn't go through. She reaches for a Fudgeo to dip in her tea but stops herself. Enough cookies for one morning. She picks a flyer out of the blue box. She's already clipped all the coupons and entered the Frigidaire contest, but maybe she missed something.

"Your patience is appreciated. Your call will be answered in turn..." Fuck off. She bangs the phone once on the counter, hard enough to satisfy but not do damage. She takes a calming sip of tea thinking maybe she should switch to herbal.

And maybe if she wrote a complaint letter to this goddamn phone company for keeping her holding so goddamn long, she'd get a free month or two long distance. Official complaining was an art passed down from her mother, who was an expert at finding eggshells, tiny stones, or long, black, "suspiciously Chinese" hair in restaurant meals. As a result they rarely ate in the same restaurant twice. She still wonders where her mother got those hairs. If Mom was in especially mortifying form, meaning more than three drinks, they would end up with dessert on the house in addition to their meals.

Peggy's less public approach to complaining was to write letters – not email, email meant you weren't really upset – but real letters handwritten on good quality paper with a nice envelope and one of those address labels the diabetes association sent free in the mail. The leaky dish soap cap brought in a two-year supply. The Coffee Crisp bug, which she had to get from her sister back east where the bars are made, scored a case of sixty. She had a closet full of paper diapers after complaining to three different companies about the sticky tabs not sticking. If only she could figure out how to wrangle the big items, like a couch.

She looks at the clock on the microwave. She's been on hold for twelve minutes now. Fuck. She almost wishes Scotty would wake up, give her something more to do. When pregnant, she was warned of sleep deprivation, walking the halls at night, nursing every two hours round the clock. But from day one, her Scotty has slept a solid ten hours at night and another six during the day. A nurse at the hospital had mentioned something about hormonal bliss and falling in love for the first time. These are also things she has yet to experience. But maybe a great buildup always ends in a letdown, like how a movie can never live up to its raves. She doesn't blame Scotty that he smells off or that his head is freakishly large compared to the rest of him. (It's no wonder his neck can't hold that thing up.) It's her fault, her lack of sensibility, and she's working on it. Scotty does have beautiful sad eyes though, that seem to understand more than they should. When he's awake, he'll stare at her, unblinking, as if she's the most amazing thing between heaven and earth. It makes her nervous; makes her terrified of disappointing him.

Peggy gives the phone another good whack on the counter, then quickly checks for a dent. Damage deposit, she reminds herself, only slightly relieved there's no damage.

"All our associates are presently busy serving other customers. Your call is impor..."

She holds the phone away from her head until the Muzak comes back on. If she had kept her cashier job at the Safeway, she'd sure be busy right now. Scanning cans, doing price checks, yakking it up with customers or her bagger, Mike. But she'd given it all up, good pay too, determined to do right by Scotty. All because she read in some parent mag at the OB's that the first three years was when a child's hard-wiring got established. And that you pay later on for not "being there." And you'd keep paying, it said. She only had to think of her own childhood to believe it.

She often lay awake at night worrying whether she has the discipline, the class to be a decent mother. Do good mothers keep the radio tuned to classical music? Do they make cookies from scratch? Does it still count if you buy dough logs? Was bad mothering genetic, like alcoholism or Tourette's?

"Yeah, help you?" comes a human voice through the receiver. A man's voice.

"Oh?" Peggy starts and spills a trail of tea down Duncan's pajama shirt. "Hi." She waits for a response. "You there?"

"Go ahead."

The guy sounds pissed off. He has some attitude when she's the one who's been on hold for fifteen minutes. "Yes, well, yesterday I registered over the net with your company and thought I was connected but –"

"Go to *start*."

"Oh, wait, I'm not at my computer." She hustles over, banging her toe on the coffee table. She bites her bottom lip keeping the word fuck to a sustained Ffff... "Okay, ready."

The guy on the other end says nothing until she clicks on start and says, "Done."

"Go to *dial-up networking*," he reels off.

"Okay."

"Change the first number to your registered password." His voice is a lot more tart than Ms. Mayonnaise's. Mr. Mustard, she'll call him.

"I had chosen two pass –"

"The first."

She types in Scotty.

"Next." He sounds as bored as she feels.

"Next? What's next?" she asks before seeing the word *next* in a box at the bottom of the screen. He hasn't responded to her confusion. She presses *next*. God, he's glib. She wants to threaten to take her business elsewhere, report him to his superiors. As if he'd care.

"Type STHP where the cursor's flashing."

She does.

"*Next*."

She presses *next*.

"Answer no to the third line."

"The one about having a direct access code?"

She thinks she hears him sigh.

"You think I'm an idiot?" she asks, accusingly.

There's a weighted pause. She'll kill him if he says yes.

"No," comes the deadpan voice, with what Peggy thinks is a flicker of amusement.

"Good choice," she says, catching the reflection of her smile in the monitor screen.

"Hold on, I have to go into the wizard."

"Into the wizard?" she repeats, but he's gone.

Her living room's greeny grey walls, a colour that looked great in a *Martha* magazine, rise into focus. Then the marshmallow couch and chair they inherited from Duncan's parents' rec room, grey and yellow plaid with the country-style frame. Fuck, she hates them. She recently entered a contest that entitles the winner to a living room set of one's choice. There're always those no payments, no interest for two years deals but Duncan doesn't trust them. With only one of them working, they can't afford to go out to a movie, much less buy furniture.

She checks the time on the screen. Eleven twenty-one. Duncan will be home in six hours. How she used to look forward to seeing him, her prince, who would rescue her from her boredom. But lately the evenings are as dull as her days. Dinner in front of the news then Duncan challenging her to "best out of three" Yahtzee. He holds Scotty for her and snacks in front of the TV 'til it's time to head upstairs, presses Billy's red button and laughs all the way to bed. Where he goes to sleep. God, how long's it been since he's tried to touch her? So goddamn nervous since the baby. Maybe he's turned off. All this flabby skin around what she used to consider a waist. Stretch marks like purple lightning. Or maybe he's intimidated by the size of her breasts and how they shot off like a couple of fireboats that one time they did do it. Her sister said she had a boyfriend who was so turned on when she had milk that he nursed as much as the baby. But Duncan looks at her as though she's some kind of Madonna. Which is too bad because, for some weird reason, she's hornier than ever. Nobody at the hospital ever mentioned that possibility.

"Yeah," comes the slacker voice back from the wizard. "*Exit* and go to *My Computer*."

She follows more apathetic commands. She doesn't really mind his deadpan tone. It sounds deep, a little dark.

"I can tell you love your job," she says.

There's a short gap.

"No."

"Duh," she says, speaking his language now.

He continues on, nonplussed. He's a decent guy, Peggy decides, and she pictures him: headset over brown wavy hair, an expensive cut, combed through this morning with his fingers. Lanky body draped in a swively office chair. Narrow but well-formed chest and good shoulders under a baggy T-shirt — no logos. He's too cool for logos. With one hand on the mouse, his legs are splayed. He's wearing black jeans with a button-up fly. Sexy, those old style buttons. Actually he's quite sophisticated, even been to Europe, and this job is way beneath him. He just needs cash to pay for some good dope and the upcoming week at Whistler with his friends. His mother stayed at home and spoiled him rotten, baked a lot of cookies from scratch, but he has perfect teeth since his father's a dentist. Peggy admires good teeth. Her own are bruised black with fillings with one molar missing since it was too far gone. She's made herself a promise that Scotty will visit the dentist twice a year.

"Type *36NP1*."

"Okay."

"Now area code plus phone."

"You have any privacy there?" She types her number.

"Nylon partitions. *Next*."

How I'd love to shake this guy up. She clicks at the screen.

"Password again."

Mr. Don't-Give-a-Shit should understand he's speaking to a flesh and blood person here, who's never been to Whistler.

"Answer *no, yes, yes* and press *next.*"

Who's never skied in her life.

"Now go to *file.*"

"You have a sexy voice." She says it slowly, putting on her best, then runs a hand over her unwashed hair. There's a pause but she can tell he's more upright in his chair. "Ever done it on the phone?" she just tosses out. Her living room with its ugly furniture fades away. She's young and beautiful.

A longer pause.

"This call is being monitored," he says.

"And you care?" She feels his blue, no, green eyes come into focus. She's gaining ground.

"You're alone...and horny?" His husky whisper has underground life.

"And wet," she says and his breath lets go into the phone. There's a squeak of wheels and she pictures him sliding his chair under his laptop to lean forward onto one elbow.

"I've gone hard," he breathes.

"Big and hard," she echoes.

"Your nipples...are your nipples pushing against your shirt?"

The tremor in his voice sends a snake down her spine.

"Yes."

"Rub your hands over them," he orders.

Oh, she does like being told what to do. She slips her hand under the elastic of Duncan's pajama pants and her full breasts start to leak through her shirt. "Mmm...and you, are you treating yourself well?"

"Oh, yes." The words stick in his throat.

"You would feel so good," Peggy says, her eyes closing as her joints ease open.

"Now, take off your...panties," he stutters, "and I want you to straddle my...cock, real slow."

Peggy suddenly hears Scotty howling upstairs. She jerks upright, looks at the monitor. What? The light's off. She forgot to turn it on? How long has he been crying?

"I gotta go," she says, hears him huff into his head-set, ready to blow the house down. She hangs up.

Hurrying upstairs, Peggy's shoulder knocks Billy the Big Mouthed Bass, sends it crashing to the floor and down a couple of steps. Hope I broke the stupid thing, she thinks, rushing along to the "nursery" as she's taken to calling it. Scotty's on his back, a helpless turtle, limbs stiff and shaking. His face is red and tear-stained as he hiccups for air between screams.

"It's okay, mama's here. It's okay." She lifts him out of the crib and moves to the rocker. "Shh, it's okay." Her hands are trembling as she unhooks her nursing bra. He's too distressed to take the nipple and the milk drips into his eye. He blinks wildly. "C'mon." She directs the milk spray into his mouth. "Num num time."

He's staring at her now as if afraid to blink in case she'll disappear. She knows the day will come when those eyes won't want to look at her ever again. She looks away, at the animal mobile jiggling in a slow circle over his crib. She used cardboard and pastel-coloured felt, traced the animal shapes from a library book. The damn thing took her two days.

Scotty calms enough to latch on and his crying cuts short. Now Peggy can hear the irritating fish serenading them from the stairwell. "Take me to the river," thump, thump, thump, "dump me in the water."

White-trash mother. What was she thinking? And she's still not connected to Nexus. Her armpits burn as her milk lets down. Damn, she'll have to call the place back. Be on hold for another fifteen minutes. Scotty gulps back milk and his eyelids flutter dully, threatening to close.

She strains her memory – did Mr. Mustard ever mention his name?

Breaking Things

NEARLY EVERY BLACK PLASTIC CHAIR IN the hospital's small waiting room is taken. Deb thinks of the room as a holding tank, and all those present criminals abetting a crime. Hot air from an overhead vent breathes down her neck. It's five below outside, a prediction of snow. She knocks on the office window and the nurse swivels to face her, slides back the glass window.

"Can you tell me how much longer?"

"Dear, the doctor's a little late. He'll be here soon." The nurse's smile is perfectly horizontal, a long dash, her lips as pale as her face. "Just have a seat and relax." She slides the window back into place and turns to the other nurse.

Deb watches them exchange words, flip through papers, tug at their ghostly stockings. Just another day on the job.

She goes and sits back down beside Noah, who's reading *Dirt Bike Fever*. He owns a bike of his own and, in summer, she rides on the back, clinging to him all the way to his parents' house on the South Shore. Their summer house.

Her eyes trace the green baseboard around the room, coming to a stop underneath the nurses' window where a new square of drywall's been installed. It's taped and filled but not painted, the colour a pasty gray alongside its clean white neighbours. A three-foot piece of green molding is missing along its base. Why hasn't that been taken care of? Wouldn't take ten minutes. She mentally paints the wall a flawless white, using an edger first, then a roller. Then saws a strip of molding pencilled off to size, some sage green paint, a couple of finishing nails. Bang, bang, all fixed.

Without looking at her, Noah strokes her arm, just once, before returning to his magazine. Noah is younger than her by five years, nineteen to her twenty-four. She knows this is hard for him, but not that hard. They met at a party when he was seventeen – his expensive clothes and general confidence made him seem older. His dark curly hair was cut to perfection, and funny lines kept emerging from between the sexiest lips she'd ever seen. There's something about Jewish men, something subversive that turns her on.

They have difference in common. Noah lives off a trust fund, goes to Dalhousie's King's College, Oxford's distant cousin, and plans to go into law. Deb is a full-time waitress who's terminally poor because she spends all her money on modern dance classes: Limon with a little Cunningham thrown in. Noah calls her passion for dance "a short-term" plan. She has no long-term plans.

They also share an intense sexual attraction. Somehow they fit each other's unspoken fantasy – the objectified older woman and the disdainful younger man – and the sex is pornographic. Deb's roommate refers to Noah as Deb's addiction. "How's the addiction?" she asks, and Deb shakes her hand as if it's on fire.

She looks around the waiting room at the other girls. Women really, all in their twenties, though maybe the gabby one in the corner is more like eighteen. No matter, she thinks of them all as girls, herself included. Naive dumb girls who confuse sex with love and love with happiness. How else has she ended up puking several times a day and waiting for her insides to be vacuumed? Her womb to be vacuumed. The word *womb* sounds like wound, only sadder.

This hospital "procedure" happens once a week on Thursday mornings. Deb had dragged herself and Noah out of bed at six in the morning last week, too, pretending to all concerned that it was her scheduled Thursday. She was desperate to get it out and over with before Christmas. She claimed it was the hospital's mistake, not hers, tried crying, said she couldn't keep any food down, couldn't sleep. The unruffled nurse said Deb wasn't far enough along for the ultrasound to detect things properly, gave her some Gravol and sent her home.

She had to make up an excuse to her parents about why she couldn't bus the five hours from Halifax to Fredericton for Christmas. "Noah really wants me to spend Christmas with his family this year," she'd said, then ignored their puzzlement over this sudden Jewish interest in Christmas. She quickly added that she was in rehearsal for a First Night Performance, her first solo, had choreographed it herself. That part was true, except for the fact that she had to opt out of the show. (She had really wanted Noah to see it, prove to him that though she may not have the talent to make a living at dance, she can still make an impression.) She had lied to the other dancers as well, telling them she couldn't get off work, and now they were totally pissed at her. The irony is she hates lying. Lying is instant loneliness. But you don't share your shame with the people you care for. You tuck shame in the back of your closet, out of sight, and hope it'll eventually go away. Or that when you do find it, years later, it will have somehow shrunk to something gray and unrecognizable.

"Look at this picture of Brad and Angie," the gabby one says to her friend, yet loud enough for every ear in the room. "She's ten times prettier than Jennifer A. And so much cooler." Her tone is self-assured, in the know. "Brad has to get over this short hair phase."

Her friend nods, her head bouncing loosely as if her neck needs tightening, then resumes staring at the floor.

Angelina Jolie. When Deb first told Noah she though she might be pregnant, they were at the movies, the lights seconds from going down. It starred Jolie and her computer enhanced breasts. Those breasts were the reason Noah wanted to see it. (Noah's a breast man all the way, a breast boy.) He was obsessed with Deb's breasts. Grade A, he called them, like they might be cooked and eaten. He was sipping orange pop through a straw when she told him, eyes fixed on the blank screen with a child's anticipation.

"Well, it's not hard to get an abortion," he said between swallows. The lights began to dim and she saw his knee start jiggling, bouncing off his heel the way it did when he was nervous. When she put her hand on it, he crossed it over his other leg.

One of the nurses steps out of her safe room and instantly magnetizes every eye in the room. This one has a ruddy complexion, a storm of short gray curls on her head. She's built low to the ground, compact as a box hedge. Standing with her feet together – her chunky legs one solid, reassuring stem – she does roll call. Deb watches as each girl dares acknowledge her existence. Two of the girls appear to be here alone. One of them is rummaging in her purse when her name's called and lifts two lazy fingers in answer. A crumpled peace sign. She pulls out a purple packet of Hubba Bubba gum. The other solo girl raises a hand while stifling a yawn with the other. Are they really so indifferent? Granted they're all tired, considering their condition and the hour they got up. The wall clock inside the nurse's station reads eight thirty. They've been waiting an hour and a half.

The loud girl's name is called and, not bothering to look up from her magazine, she agitates the air with a fist. Another girl, sitting with what looks like her mother or aunt, says "yes" in a child's voice. The next girl just nods solemnly. Like Deb, she's here with her boyfriend, only they're holding hands and sitting so close their shoulders touch.

They have a mature relationship, thinks Deb. This girl could be a woman. Yes, she would call her a woman and her boyfriend, a man. Both look twenty-five easy, grad students maybe, this pregnancy in the way of ambition, diplomas, smart jobs.

"Deborah Gaines?"

"I'm here," she blurts.

"It shouldn't be much longer," the nurse says and goes back behind her glass.

Deb's eyes speed along the green molding to stop dead at the unfinished drywall. Her stomach begins its routine of hollowing out with hunger before filling with a sourness that triggers her reflux. Without a word to Noah, she's out of her seat and hurrying into the bathroom, where she runs the tap water to cover the sound of heaving into the toilet. Since she was required to fast from midnight on, only air explodes into the bowl.

"You all right?" comes Noah's quiet voice at the door.

She coughs. "Yes."

She knows that in coming with her today, Noah's just trying to do the right thing. She respects him for it, but thinks now that she'd prefer to be alone.

As she returns to the waiting room, sunlight is streaming in through the room's one small window. The light makes a neat rectangle in the middle of the floor. She imagines it as a door and, like Alice in Wonderland, she could fall through and everything would be different. On the way to her seat, she steps carefully into the box of light, eyes closing, hesitates a second before continuing. Back in her seat, she leans her tired head against the wall.

The two solo girls have struck up a conversation, the sleepy one laughing out loud over something the gum chewer said. The mother and daughter team are quietly planning "Uncle Bobby's birthday."

"The air is so dry in here," she says to Noah, who shrugs. "And warm." She takes off her sweater.

The mature couple focus on textbooks propped on crossed knees so they can still hold hands. Absorbed in her mag, the gabby one whistles mindless through her teeth. Despite the loose sweater, Deb can tell she's well past the seven to ten week mark. Who's she fooling? Over ten weeks you have to go in for a D and C: dilation and, what's the C word?, something that means scraping. If you're closer to twenty weeks, the law makes you go full term.

"You better?" Noah asks, his eyes briefly meeting hers.

"Not really."

He gives her arm a squeeze. She wants him to hold her, to sing in her ear the way he does when they're in his little car, music filling their senses. It makes her weak when he sings to her like that.

"I'm going to get a muffin," he says and bounds out of his chair. "Want something?"

Deb cocks her head, giving him the look.

"Oh yeah, forgot. Back in a sec."

She watches him leave, thinking how she's always been slightly afraid of him. He's intense and unpredictable, an alpha-male puppy who happens to be full-grown. She wants to blame this whole thing on him. He's the one who slept with that married woman when visiting his grandparents in Boston. And with that girl in his class, that young thing with the army boots. She can only guess at the affairs she doesn't know about. Her own affair, if she can even call it that, lasted an hour. Just long enough to regain some pride and end up here. She picks up a rumpled *People* magazine. Royals litter the magazine's cover as if they're up for auction. She attempts to read about the girl Prince William's been seeing and her eyes swerve with nausea. She takes a deep breath. If Noah knew the truth about this pregnancy, he very well might hurt her.

There had been a moment of curious joy there in the mall washroom as the unmistakable blue line rose in the little plastic window. It seemed miraculous that her body was capable of such sacred magic. It was awe-inspiring. She tries to conjure her lover's face, but, for the moment, can only manage his eyes: round, wide set, green with a splatter of gold.

Noah returns with a lollipop stick protruding from his lips.

"I got you one for later." He holds up a purple wrapped Tootsie pop.

She smiles weakly.

"I have to go out in the hall," she announces, unable to sit in here a moment longer with these *laissez faire* girls.

Moving makes the nausea worse so Deb seeks out the empty gurney down the hall. As she lies down, her calves twitch with odd sparking sensations. It's something they've been doing lately whenever she lies down, especially at night when she's trying to get to sleep. She lays her hands over her still taut dancer's belly and is suddenly afraid. What if something goes wrong? Or what if it doesn't work? Or she's messed up for having babies later on? She's always wanted children some day.

Somehow she knows this kidney bean-shaped thing claiming her body is a boy. As hard as she tries, she can't help but picture it as a curled up, miniature eight-year-old boy. She imagines him shy, fair-haired, kind of studious, or that he would be all these things if she wasn't about to send him back into the void. She's so sorry. So very sorry.

She recalls that the father's hair was blond, straight, long enough that he kept tucking one side behind his ear. He had been gentleman enough to walk her home after, or to what she claimed was home. After a peck on her cheek he'd smiled slyly then said good-night. He had a dark hole in his smile where a molar was missing just behind his eye tooth.

"Hi there. Got a cigarette?"

Noah has followed her into the hall, and like a proper teen, he's making jokes.

"Ugh, even the thought."

Deb's a social smoker but hasn't been able to go near a smoke since the nausea hit three weeks ago. Noah doesn't smoke, he chain-sucks lollipops. Now the other nurse, the pale one, appears beside a far door. She is tall and narrow, a young sapling, with a limp brown ponytail.

"Deborah?"

"Me?" Deb sits up on the gurney too quickly and her head dips woozily.

"I've just phoned the doctor and apparently he's forgotten it was his turn this week. He apologizes and will be along shortly."

"Great. Okay. Thanks."

The nurse ducks back in her office and Deb moans and lies back down. Great? Okay? Thanks? Why is she so fucking accommodating all the time? She should have said, "That's not acceptable and I want a formal apology. In writing."

Maybe the doctor's a moralist and is always late on his turn, hoping to teach those dirty girls a lesson. Maybe he's a sadist. In any case, she's dependent on him. Has no choice but to entrust her body, her reproductive organs and thus her future maternity to a total stranger.

"God, those girls in there seem so casual. Isn't anybody else freaking out, even a little?" she demands of Noah. He looks at her nervously.

"I'll take you home after this is over and tuck you into bed," he offers, his lollipop pushing out his cheek like a tumour. "Then I've promised Tom I'd go shopping with him. Maybe get that leather jacket at *Ground Zero*."

Deb shops at Second Hand Rose or trades clothes with friends. The one time she and Noah took a trip to Boston together and were going to stay at his grandparents, he took her to Harrod's for Women first and bought her an outfit – skirt, shirt, vest and belt – just on a whim. The belt alone, made from real alligator, cost over two hundred dollars. She'd felt like Eliza Doolittle.

She pulls up her knees, curls into the fetal position, the bean's position. One being curled around another. She imagines her own mother curled around her back, her grandmother behind her mother, and on and on. She grinds her cheek against the starchy white sheet. Why is birth control always the girl's responsibility? As if females aren't equally reckless, equally horny? Why didn't she speak up and tell him she didn't have protection? Why not? Why?

A blur of time passes. Noah is telling her about the courses he's taking next term when footsteps force Deb to sit up. A guy with wire-rim glasses, long sideburns and sleek black coat comes striding down the hall. He gives Deb and Noah a disapproving glance before turning in at the same door the nurse came out of. He's young, maybe thirty-five.

"I bet that's him," says Noah.

Deb's empty stomach seems to turn over.

"Maybe we should go back in."

She groans herself down from the high bed, slides her hands up over her hair and down her neck, petting herself.

Though she hadn't been first on the roll call list, the girl that's here with her mother is called in. As if having a condoning relative here awards her status. As if this girl's crime and hers alone is an honest mistake, an accident, caught from a toilet seat. Or maybe they're simply mixing people up which means Deb won't be last after all. It's pretty obvious she's suffering the most here. Outwardly anyway. That should count for something.

With a squeeze from her auntie's hand, the called girl stands up, a tilted smile to her round, babyish face. Her cherubic cheeks have turned a pretty pink. The nurse hands her a faded blue dressing gown and ushers her through the double doors that separate the waiting room from whatever lies beyond.

Five minutes later the waiting room is stone quiet. Deb knows she isn't alone in listening, hard, for sounds of pain. She hears nothing. Can it be that simple? Her eyes race along the green baseboard and jump the gap to continue along the other side.

"Mmm, look at this dress," Gabby says to her friend. "Bad shoes, though. God, when you have as much money as her, you think you could buy some taste. You could hire someone with taste." The friend gnaws at the skin around her nail.

Deb gets up again, to stand by the window. The sun is gone and the December sky's now a solid cast of white. The occasional snowflake drifts tentatively to the ground, scout flakes, she thinks, checking to see if it's safe before calling the others. She starts to count cars in the parking lot. Red ones first. Blue next. She's dying to open the window, just a crack, craves the cold air. But no one else is complaining. Eleven red cars, including maroon.

Before the first girl returns, a second girl's called. It's Gabby's turn. Her name is actually Tamara Gainer. She stands and tosses her mag behind her without looking. It hits her friend in the chest and slips to the floor before any reflexes kick in. There's a determined ignorance to Gabby's face when the nurse does a double take at the size of her gut. Gabby stands taller, squares off her shoulders as if daring the nurse to say something. It's pathetic to watch. Her breasts are a good size too, swollen with hormones, and her cleavage eases out the top of the v-neck sweater. Deb sees Noah eyeing them, his cheeks indenting as he sucks harder on his Tootsie pop, her Tootsie pop, the first one finished. Deb returns to her cars.

Sixteen blue, she counts. Twelve black. Though from up here on the third floor, she can't tell if some of those are really navy or black cherry. Her sister has a black cherry van. A black cherry van, two kids and a faithful husband who cooks.

Yellow. There's Noah's car, an Alpha Romeo, *Spider Veloce*. So like him, that car. Sometimes they hold hands while they drive. Noah will keep her hand in his while he shifts the beautiful mahogany gearshift. The dashboard too is mahogany, a glossy burnt red. She loves feeling like he can't let her go. His car's more of a custard colour than real yellow. Three yellow, one custard.

Deb's hoping to glimpse the after face of the first girl, but the nurse tells the girl's auntie to bring their coats and then escorts her through the double doors. Gabby, who hasn't been gone very long, comes striding back into the waiting room, a sight-lessness to her eyes and a white sheet of paper crack-ling in her fist. She grabs up her coat, crushing the paper underneath and heads for the door. Her bovine friend hustles after her. The tension in the room goes up a notch. One of our own has failed in the group mission: To rid ourselves of our fateful mistakes. Two down, four to go. Twenty-one green cars, mostly silver green, which was a popular colour a few years back.

TWO MORE GIRLS GO IN, one coming out almost as quickly as Gabby. It's the gum chewer, her jaw now rigid. She's close to tears. Like Gabby, she also must be too far along, conception dates confused or perhaps she's simply a fan of denial. Deb watches the girl struggle with her coat then carefully fold the hand-out in half and in half again before slipping it into her pocket. Deb feels the girl's disappointment like a virus and her stomach threatens to heave again. She wills it away. There isn't time to puke, she could be called next. White, lots of white cars, ridges of blackened snow clumped along the base of their chassis. Cargoyles her father calls them. Eight, nine, ten... There was a light dusting of snow over the cemetery grounds that night and her lover had spread his coat on the ground. It was cold so they kept most of their clothes on.

The girl with the boyfriend, the woman, is called next, which means Deb is still last on the list.

The woman and her man friend stand up together, hand in hand.

"I'm going in with her," he explains to the nurse. His voice is deep.

Deb looks at Noah, who pretends to be absorbed in his magazine. His lollipop, her lollipop, is long gone but he continues to tongue the stick, flipping it side to side. She wouldn't want him in there anyway. She needs to be anonymous in order to disappear. She can never disappear with Noah around, always has to be on her guard, make sure he isn't being disappointed in her or losing interest.

The clock says eleven ten. She's been waiting now over four hours. Her stomach is screaming at her for food. Everyone's left the waiting room, so she turns the handle on the window and pushes it open just enough for cold air to spirit in around the edges. She inhales gratefully, then realizes that past the parking lot and across South Street she can see a corner of the cemetery's wrought iron fence. They had used a large headstone to block the wind. It was dark, hushed, the distant sound of cars turning up slush. They had met only two hours earlier, shared the last available table at Claire's Coffee Emporium. She had walked out on a fight with Noah, who hadn't come home the night before. Nor had he called. She'd waited by the phone, hadn't slept. He was with friends, he said, was too late to call. When she asked who he slept with, he didn't answer. In her jealous rage, she had broken her favourite bottle from her blue glass collection, heaved it against her kitchen stove. She always broke something she valued, and had to wonder who she was trying to punish. It took a half hour to clean up the fine shards.

Through the opened window, she hears it. A girl's cry, bitten back. She stops breathing to listen. Was that a gasping sound? Pain? Or grief? Both? Those two won't be able to stay together after this, she thinks nervously. Despite their clear-eyed logics, they won't be able to make love without turning their heads. The snow has decided it's safe to come out and falls in straight lines like beaded curtains. Only these wouldn't make any sound. She closes her eyes.

He was in town for a wedding. She didn't ask whose. She felt oddly at ease with him, like he was some long-lost younger brother. "Wanna fuck?" she'd said to him. Just like that. Wanna fuck? She was out of her mind with lack of sleep. She'd undone the top button of her blouse, pulled it aside to flash the cleavage Noah coveted. The guy had glanced upward as if to thank the Lord above. Laughing and reckless, she had run down the street and into the cemetery. He chased after her, tackling her gently, cradling her length to the ground. She wouldn't let him tell her his name.

"Deborah Gaines?" calls the nurse, the box hedge.

Deb turns in amazement, coughing her lungs into action. "Me?" Already? She glances back out the window and runs a hand over her hair. How many white cars?

Noah is nodding his head encouragingly. She smiles as walks toward the nurse's extended hand holding the neatly folded blue gown. She glances down at the missing baseboard's dirty gray gap. The nurse turns to lead the way but Deb's feet can't move.

"I can't go in there," she whispers.

"Have you changed your mind, dear? You're allowed to change your mind." The practical mouth tips as the nurse angles her head to look in Deb's face, as if to decide for her.

"I...I just...need...something for the pain." The words jerk from her tongue.

"Yes, dear. That's fine." With an urgent flutter of her hand, she summons the other nurse behind the glass.

Noah has stood up by his chair but stays where he is. After a moment he sits back down, measured concern leaning him forward, the stick between his lips an opaque thermometer.

A pleated cup holding a pill is placed in one of Deb's hands and a flowered Dixie cup of water in the other.

"There we are; drink up and we'll go put on the gown together. You're going to be fine." The nurse's emotionless voice is pleasantly numbing. Deb badly wants to have her head petted just once, by someone else's hand.

In the dressing room, the nurse silently ties the gown's closures into bows. Deb needs to say it in front of someone. Needs to have a witness.

"I'm breaking up with Noah," she announces to the wall of hooks, her dangling jeans, the white flag of underwear sticking out of the pocket. "I'm starting fresh. A clean slate."

THE PILL DISTANCES EVERYTHING: the doctor's face...the nurses, on either side, holding her shaking legs apart...their instructions not to move a muscle...the hidden knot in her being forced to open...a growling machine...all those dumb girls swallowing their fear...the grey drywall which she mentally paints using an edger first, then a roller...a strip of molding pencilled off to size ...some sage green paint, a couple of finishing nails. Bang. Bang...Bang, Bang, Bang, Bang, Bang –

A voice behind her head is urging her to "hush."

Raising Blood

J ON DIDN'T MEAN TO HAVE SEX WITH THE NEW systems analyst, the woman who, more or less, replaced his and six other jobs. The situation just got away from him is all. Never in ten years of marriage had he even considered straying. It was the night of Hydro's "thanks and get lost" party. He had been liberal with the punch and while filling up yet again, she was there, waiting her turn.

"Here, allow me, Software," he said, taking her cup. The term fit her cumulus curves, her whitish-pink flesh and seemed to snag her imagination too. Under the red light cast by the Christmas bulbs someone had strung haphazardly around the walls, the systems analyst looked at him anew.

"You speak French?" she asked, too close to his ear.

"Un petit peu," he said, too close to hers. They clinked glasses. "Salut." He might or might not have winked.

He watched her drain her glass in one go and then she waited, one eyebrow cocked, as he drained his. She took his glass and hers, plunked them down on the table, hooked her arm in his and pulled him onto the dance floor. Her generous hips rolled, her breasts swayed, while he, who didn't dance, marched around her and flapped his elbows. She laughed, delighted, and did it too. Jon was flattered by the attention, surprised too. Women rarely paid him much attention anymore. He had a bit of a paunch, yes, but mostly he blamed his hairline. For the last five years his hair had crept steadily away from his eyebrows to create the forehead, that kept on going. Looking in his bathroom mirror was like looking into those funhouse mirrors at amusement parks, his face stretched weirdly out of proportion. His wife, Valerie, called it a nobleman's forehead, yet never failed to buy him a new hat when away on business. She was away on business the night of the party.

His boss, now his former boss, stood on the sidelines watching him and Software dance. Jon thought the man looked jealous and, pleased by this mini-revenge, had slid one hand over Software's hip. But he'd never meant to sleep with her. He'd simply had too much punch. And what scoundrel brought Marvin Gaye's greatest hits?

Software, with her high-riding breasts and mysterious tunnel of cleavage, had continued to follow him right to his car. This doughy sculpture, Jon found out in the master bedroom of his townhouse, was buoyed up by a bra stuffed with black half moons filled with water. "Lily pads," she called them with a random toss over her shoulder. Bra gone, the nipples of her large, well-hung breasts now eyed the wood floor. Hands raised in surrender, she broke into a blue velvet chorus of "Heard it through the Grapevine," the pendulous ball of her hips kicking side to side. Valerie's narrow hips never kicked. His Valerie, recent junior partner in her law firm, who, even before the layoff, was making more money than him, listened to opera.

Jon felt they should do it somewhere other than his marriage bed. Like in the shower, where all scents and fluids would hide themselves down the drain. Or in the room furthest from the bedroom: the car. But Software took one look at his and Valerie's king-sized nest and crawled onto it, on all fours, nothing more than a string covering her terrible thing. He had enough sense to pull back the antique quilt, the top sheet even. Valerie had purchased this particular set of sheets yesterday before leaving for her weekend conference. "They're pure Egyptian cotton," she'd told him excitedly, "handmade lace and a 600 thread count."

"Isn't that something," he'd said, admiringly, though he hadn't a clue what thread count meant, besides expensive.

Now, here he was, kneeling in the middle of Valerie's five hundred dollar white sheets, Software's rear end a brilliant moon under his hands, her spine a swayed white bridge. She'd gone still, small gasps of air escaping her nose. His guilt was in its final throes, reduced to something single celled when Software began muttering through what sounded like clenched teeth. "Stupid" and "bitch" were the only words he caught before the top of his head strained for the ceiling fixture. Together they collapsed in a panting mess of weakened joints. Software began laughing like a schoolgirl. An infectious, manic laugh that got Jon laughing too. Their bodies quaked together and he laughed harder still as he balanced her jostling breasts in his opened palms, weighing which was heavier. Beyond his own dying laughter, he heard what sounded like anguish. Software rolled away from his touch, looked at him with weeping, mascara-bruised eyes and buried her face in the freshly dressed pillow.

"Are you alright?" asked Jon.

She lifted her face off the pillow and slammed it down. And again. And again.

Jon inched over in the bed and sat up. Picking up in speed and violence, her headbanging was accompanied by a whimpering snarl. This bizarre post-coital response continued for what might be a bug's lifetime before she lunged off the bed, grabbed up her tiny hill of clothes and stumbled into the washroom. He winced as she slammed the bathroom door. What had he done? He thought of his reasonable Valerie, who liked to snuggle after sex and give him a synopsis of her latest book club novel. He fell back on his pillow with a groan of remorse. He was exhausted now, spent, and wanted nothing more than to close his weary eyes and sleep. In fact, he couldn't keep his eyes open. He rolled onto his side and his knee hit a wet spot. The wet spot. Except it was more than wet. He groaned and sat up again. What the...? Ew. Smack in the middle of the supremely fitted Egyptian sheet was a ruddy red stain the size of a cantaloupe. It was as if a giant raindrop, a giant blood drop, had fallen from the sky when he wasn't looking.

He lunged for the box of Kleenex beside the bed and frantically piled one fly-away tissue on top of another to absorb this unstable woman's blood. He was desperate to rip the sheet off, barge into the washroom and plunge the stain under running water. But she was in there. He didn't want to stir that pot again. He piled on more tissues and gingerly pressed down. He hated the sight of blood. He was a person who opted to lie down for blood tests. Valerie always respected his sensibilities and was fastidious about keeping her sanitary things in a separate pink garbage can hidden under the sink. Jon preferred to think of his wife, and women in general, as periodically dispensing the kind of blood he stole sips from as an altar boy. Say a full-bodied Cabernet or Shiraz.

Software emerged from the bathroom fully dressed and combed, one breast distinctly higher than the other. She stood in the doorway, cleared her throat of what sounded like an orchestra of phlegm, then inhaled deeply through her nose.

"This never happened," she said, composed and businesslike, then started toward the bedroom door.

His crotch carefully covered, one casual hand on a mound of tissues, Jon said nothing, hoping this would expedite her leaving. To his alarm, she stopped in the doorway, turned and aimed one finger in his general direction.

"And no, I'm not going to Paris with you."

Paris?

He waited, heard the front door click shut, then wrenched the elasticized sheet off the bed. Under a scalding shower, he muscled the bar of Ivory into the sheet, dropped it on the bathtub floor and stomped on it. Pink water wheeled down the drain.

Ten minutes later, he stared at the darkening red spot between his feet. The stain was mocking him now, as if the harder he scrubbed the more it hung on. "Out, out damn spot," he pleaded to the ceiling. At least it was more wine coloured now, he told himself, leaving it to soak. He put on his robe and went to make himself some comfort food: peanut butter toast and hot milk with honey and a dollop of butter.

When he returned, the spot was unchanged. In fact it looked like it might have grown. What was he doing wrong? Defeated and exhausted, he sat down on the toilet and looked longingly out at the stripped bed. A red blotch on the mattress pad stared back at him. Shit. He dragged himself over to the bed and stared down the stain. It was shaped just like Hungary.

He removed the pad and dared to squint at the mattress beneath. It took him twenty minutes, what with pausing for breath, to flip the monster over and hide the button-sized brown stain. One gone, two to go, he thought, and put the pad and sheet into the washer with hot water and bleach.

"That's what bleach is for," he said aloud, "to take out colour." Valerie always put bleach in with "the whites" as she called them. She wouldn't be back until tomorrow evening. He had time.

He remade the padless bed with old sheets, climbed aboard and fell asleep to the soothing chug of the washing machine.

HE WOKE THE NEXT MORNING with his tongue pasted to the roof of his mouth. It made a dry sucking sound as he pulled it away and last night came flooding back, along with a ripping headache. After three Aspirin and a double water, he went to check the bedding in the washer. The mattress pad he could replace, but the sheet was another story. Even if he could figure out which store it came from, he certainly didn't want to spend another half-thou on sheets when he'd seen Valerie raise the nosebleed stains on his favourite golf shirt in a matter of seconds.

"I swear to promise it will never happen again," he said as he reached into the washing machine. "Not in a million years. I learned my lesson and I love and appreciate my marriage more than ever. I will never, cross my heart, cheat on Valerie again." He hauled out the sheet.

"Looks damn white," he muttered, spreading the cool wetness across his arms. "Good, good...not good." The stain had paled slightly but the spot's outline was somehow darker, almost black. "Oh god."

He looked up poison control in the phone book.

"State your name and emergency," came a woman's voice.

"Jon Ayle here, and well, it's an emergency that's left blood on my white sheet."

"And..." she sounded impatient.

"Can you tell me how you get out bloodstains."

"Sir, this is not what our service is for."

"Please," he said tragically.

"Cold water. Not warm. Warm water will set the stain." She hung up.

"What about hot water?" he asked the dial tone.

His headache begin to throb. "Now what am I...I know," he said brightly. "It's *my* blood."

Midway down the sheet the way it was, the blood could easily have come from his knee, a nasty cut from a nasty fall, which had reopened again in the night. Not his fault that it soaked right through the bandage. And if his knee looked bad enough, Valerie might feel sorrier for him than for her new sheet.

Encouraged, Jon went into the bedroom and dug out a pair of khaki shorts, a wool sweater and thick socks. It was March after all, not exactly shorts weather. He had skinned his knees on a regular basis as a kid, running down the sidewalk, a spontaneous trip on the rubber soles of his Keds. The skin would be scraped away, the blood rising before his brain could even register the pain.

Outside he squatted on the cement steps of his townhouse and ran a finger along the steps' grainy nap. A good hard trip up these stairs should do it, he thought, punching the air with his fist.

His neighbour, Mrs. Torquay, poked her head out her front door to retrieve her Sunday paper. Under a brown nylon net, she wore curlers the size of cans. Her head looked enormous on top of her narrow body and, in her brown sweats, she looked like a giant ant.

"Good morning, Eileen," he said.

"Morning, Jon," she said, eyeing his shorts. "Is it supposed to warm up today?"

"Pants at the cleaners." He shrugged.

After Mrs. Torquay went inside, Jon waited for a car to pass by, then a truck, before trotting down the two steps and onto the walk. He turned around, took a smiling breath and jogged back towards the house. Approaching the steps, he slowed, cinched in his stomach and fell, hands catching himself, his knee gracing the cement before he lightly dragged it forward. He liked his legs – they were shapely (in a manly way) and perhaps his best feature. He examined the ghostly scrapes, waited those childhood seconds for the shiny red beads to rise forth along with the pain. Nothing.

With abandon this time, he thought, springing back up.

He strode confidently down the steps, waited until some noisy skateboarders rumbled by and then a man with a small hyper-eyed dog.

"Morning," came the man's deep baritone as his tiny dog lifted a leg to a nearby tree.

Jon smiled absently and eyeballed the steps.

"Bloody hell," the man shouted and Jon startled.

The little dog was gagging, his small spine arching in hard spasms. An absurdly loud retching came from his dime-sized throat before he puked up something green and shiny. Jon looked away.

"Come on, you," the man muttered to the dog. "Get along."

Wasn't he going to scoop that puke?

A second gagging sound sent Jon towards the steps, one eye pinching closed, urging the second to follow suit. He stopped short of the first step, knelt down on the cement landing and began to draw his knee back and forth. Scrape, scrape scrape, he thought positively, stopping when the area began to burn.

"I'm too thick-skinned," he announced. Besides, he was getting cold. He went back inside.

Jon sat in his and Valerie's copper-coloured kitchen with the blue accents. How else could he do it? The potato peeler? A paring knife? No, no, he just couldn't. Not deliberately with his own hand. He thought of that news story a few years back about a mountain climber whose arm became trapped under a boulder after he'd climbed down some impossibly steep canyon. The guy had been exploring the remote area alone, hadn't told anyone where he was headed. After several days stuck there, without food or water, he made a tourniquet out of the rubber rim of his water bottle, tied off his arm and proceeded to amputate it at the elbow joint with his pocket knife. Jon wondered if while sawing through his sinews and nerves, the man had bitten down on a rock or simply filled the canyon with the sound of hell. Supposedly the guy and his stump rappelled, one-handed, down the six-story-high canyon cliff before hiking miles for help.

"Crazy son of a bitch," said Jon, looking upward and seeing, tucked up on top of a cupboard, his Uncle Ross's wedding present.

Still unused, still plastic-wrapped inside its box, the electric carving knife was one of those must-have items of his parents' generation, right up there with the electric can opener and the electric blanket. Just a touch of the whirring blade to a bent knee, thought Jon as he pulled over a chair to stand on, and the carving knife would spin aside some skin and do the cutting for him. He wouldn't even have to look. He could lie down if he wanted. Have an antiseptic soaked bandage at the ready, slap it on, let the blood soak through and save it to show Valerie how it had leaked onto the sheet. He glanced at his watch. Her plane landed in five hours.

Sitting in the kitchen chair, bandage at the ready, Jon held the shiny serrated blade up against his knee. The thought of hitting bone made him weak and he lowered it to the soft area below the kneecap. He raised the blade in front of his face and pressed the trigger. The vibrating blade made a friendly buzz like the whirr of a hummingbird. The handle tickled his fingers.

He asked the air, "Dark meat or light?" "A leg please."

Re-establishing the blade at his knee, he rested his finger on the trigger.

"Don't think too much..." He clenched his eyes shut, "...just do it."

Hummingbird on, he gave his knee a little...tap.

"Aaagh!"

The machine clattered to the floor.

"Jesus, fuck." Jon's lower leg had gone limp.

He grabbed the bandage and, squinting, covered the wound. One second later the gauze was soaked to dripping. He couldn't feel pain yet, but glanced down and saw that where the doctor tapped his rubber reflex hammer, there was now nothing to tap. Instead of facing forward like normal, his kneecap faced the ceiling. "Ugh." Jon felt weak all over. Blood was filling the rumpled neck of his sock. He seized the nearest dishtowel, decided it was used and therefore unsanitary and tossed it away. The pain was now a searing, face-twisting burn. Blinking back tears, Jon tried to walk to where the napkins sat all high and white on the counter. His dangling leg wouldn't support weight and he hopped across the floor, freckling the beige tiles with blood. He softly pressed a wad of napkins softly up against what used to be his knee before tying a clean dish towel around it with electrician's tape. His blood, he couldn't help noticing, was a much brighter colour than Software's. Fresher, more crucial looking. He needed stitches. He needed more than stitches.

TRYING TO WORK THE GAS and brake pedals with the wrong leg emphasized his light-headedness. Why hadn't he thought to cut his left knee? As he pulled into the street, sweat beaded along his hairline. He opened the window for air, panted through the pain.

At the next corner, the car in front of him braked suddenly for a kid on a bike. Jon's dead leg instinctively went for the brake before his left scrambled over and caught just under the pedal's rubber edge. He slammed into the car's back end and jerked to a stop.

"I don't believe it." He gave the steering wheel a spank.

Jon backed away from the crumpled bumper and shattered brake lights and turned off his engine. His knee throbbed. The blood-soaked dishtowel was way past being absorbent and blood was staining the carpet of the car. His head fell back on the headrest. He couldn't walk, so whoever it was whose car he hit would have to come to him.

A minute passed. Two minutes passed. Where was he? She? From here it looked like the person he'd hit was leaning on the wheel waiting for him.

"Okay, fine. Be pissy about it."

He pulled himself out of the car, wincing at the effort, and hopped ahead. Through the window, a grey-haired man stared at him with one wide frozen eye, his face flattened against the wheel. The man's right hand batted pathetically at the door handle.

"Dear god." Jon reached for the guy's door. It was locked.

AFTER BEING GRILLED BY THE POLICE, his license and insurance papers taken away, Jon lay on a gurney in the back of an ambulance. Within touching distance, on a second gurney, the grey-haired man lay still as a corpse. There was an oxygen mask over his half-petrified face. He must have had a stroke, Jon had reasoned to the cops. They couldn't blame him for that. It was an unfortunate coincidence that his rear-ending the man provided a tiny push over that fit-to-burst edge. And he couldn't be more sorry or feel more miserable about it. The police said they'd be in touch.

"Now let's see that knee," said the ambulance attendant in a German accent so pronounced Jon had to check his face to see if he was kidding. The careful unwrapping of his knee reminded Jon of the way Valerie unwrapped presents, mindful not to tear the paper so it could be used again. He held his breath as the German tugged bits of napkin away from his cut.

"I would venture to say you have severed some major tendons," he said.

Jon suppressed a groan. Who was he to complain? At least he could still smile on both sides of his face.

"How is it that you managed to do that?" the German asked with a chuckle, as if this was all great fun.

THE EMERGENCY ROOM DOCTOR performing the operation had a shaved head and oval glasses that shrunk his eyes to piggish slits. He reminded Jon of the banjo player in *Deliverance*. One should have some sort of choice about who's sewing up your insides, he thought, as the nurse eased his head back onto the table. Her wrist had a vague scent of hand cream and he thought of Valerie. She would be landing soon, arriving home to a kitchen splattered with blood.

"I need to be home before seven," he managed to say before a rubber-edged mask covered his mouth and nose, a hazy voice instructing him to count backwards from ten.

JON WOKE GROGGY and hiccuping, hooked up to a bulbous sac of blood hanging from a metal stand. A deep ache ran the length of his leg and his armpits ached slightly. Valerie's concerned face hovered into view. When he tried to say her name, a low guttural sound rippled his lips and he burped helplessly. She turned her head to one side.

"Sorry," he said and he was. Sorry for cheating, sorry for the sheets, for severing his knee, for burping in her face. Truly sorry.

"Valerie." He groped for her hand before realizing he was already holding it.

"Jon, you had me so worried."

"Yes."

"The kitchen is a mess." She squeezed his hand.

Jon shook his head in pathetic agreement. "Was test driving damn knife and slipped."

Her cool hand stroked the hair from his forehead and he let his eyes close. It's over, he thought, my nightmare's over.

Valerie's voice slowed, "A shame you got blood on our new sheet." Her hand ceased stroking.

Jon struggled to organize his thoughts into a meaningful sequence.

"Squeamish. Had to lie down," he said weakly.

"We know how you hate the sight of blood." She removed her hand.

"Yes. Thought it had stopped bleeding. Tried to wash sheet then put old sheet back on."

Valerie said nothing.

"The weekend from hell," he said. "So glad you're back."

A nurse appeared and Valerie let go of his hand to make room. The nurse rattled his sack of blood then said something about "a little morphine."

"Will I sleep?"

"Yes, most likely." She gave Val a look of apology.

"It's fine," said Val. "We're almost finished."

After giving him a shot in his arm, the nurse went away and the morphine started its happy journey through his veins. "Oh, Val," he said, a wave of relaxation pulling him under. He let his eyes close again and reached for her hand. Her hand was oddly small and squishy. He glanced down at a black half moon shape. Software's *lily pad*.

Jon struggled to lift his head, to deny, to explain but could only stare in guilty silence.

"You balding shit," said Valerie and he felt a wrench on his wrist.

Something sprayed his arm and tiny roses began blooming on the white sheet. The tube from the needle in his arm hung free, dripping blood onto the floor. Not more blood, he thought, as the sound of footsteps moved farther and farther away.

Cold water, not hot, was his one clear thought before he fell asleep.

What Sort of Mother

IKE THEY'VE DONE EVERY SUNDAY OF THEIR married life, Nancy, Johnny and the kids are driving from Victoria to Sydney to Johnny's parents' house for dinner. Nancy goes for Johnny's sake, but feels the same annoyance and dread as she did as a child forced to attend Sunday mass. Under her mother-in-law's damning eye, she has an irrational fear of being exposed as a heathen, the one among them who doesn't believe in God and family.

"But I saw it first," whines four-year-old Charlie from the back seat. It's a high-pitch whine that sets Nancy's nerves on orange alert.

"No, I did," brays Danielle, two years older.

"Noooooo..." cries Charlie, a sickening octave higher.

"Give it to me," Danielle growls through clenched teeth.

When Nancy hears Danielle smack her brother with an open hand, she sees red, and only red. Even before Charlie can start howling, Nancy is out of her seat belt and on her knees facing the back

"Don't hit," she yells, whacking her daughter on the shoulder, hard. She remains aware enough to avoid the face. *Never, ever hit one of our children in the face*, Johnny once warned her. "Now give it to me." Danielle meekly opens her hand and surrenders a little plastic fox whose ears have been chewed off.

"You're fighting over this?" She falls back in her seat, panting.

"Calm down, Nance," says Johnny kindly, but with that slight disbelief in his voice. That disappointment.

She hears her daughter's sad whimper, her injury, and is instantly filled with self-loathing. She doesn't want to be like this. Johnny knows this is not who she is.

"Only ten more minutes to Grandmere's," he says to the kids. "How about a game?"

"I spy?" yells Charlie.

"I'm sorry," blurts Nancy, head in hand. "I'm sorry I lost it. I'm sorry I hit you, Danielle." This is her pattern. She loses her temper, then, human again, needs to apologize. But the damage is already done. 'Don't hit,' she told her daughter as she hit her. Why can't she control herself?

The kids and their father play I SPY while Nancy looks out the window, tears blurring the landscape.

FRED AND JANINE'S DRIVEWAY is bordered by a low rock wall spilling white lobelia. White tulips line the path up to their white house. White roses will bloom around the doorway come summer and the camellia bushes, also, will bloom white. White – the absence of colour – is Johnny's mother's favourite colour.

As soon as the car comes to a stop, the kids race to the front door to be the first to ring the doorbell. Danielle had positioned herself on the left side of the car to have the advantage and, as usual, reaches the door first. Charlie has yet to figure out her strategy. After she pushes the white dot, Charlie arrives breathless behind her and smacks her on the back. Don't hit, Nancy wants to say, but has lost the right.

"Ow! Mom! Charlie hit me," Nancy hears as she leans over to lift the pan of pear crumble out of the trunk. Why me? Why must they call out for me? Her purse strap slips off her shoulder and the purse tears through the foil top of the pan.

"Shit," she hisses under her breath.

"He rang it again. That's not fair," yells Danielle and Nancy straightens up to see her daughter swing her younger brother by the arm and him fall to his bum on the cement. She bites her tongue, feels the heat rise in her face. Charlie buries his face in one elbow and scream-cries.

"Do something, please," Nancy says to Johnny.

"Take it easy, guys," Johnny calls out jovially as he hurries up the path.

Johnny's mother, Janine, answers the door and throws up her hands in a dramatic pantomime. "Mon dieu?" She glances first at Nancy, to locate the blame, then sweeps outside to assist Charlie off the ground. "You poor, poor child? Grandmere will make it better?"

Though Janine's been married to an Anglo and lived in British Columbia for forty years, her French accent has only grown more distinct. And because she places her emphasis on the last syllable of each sentence, everything out of her mouth sounds like a rhetorical question. Her name is pronounced Zhanine and she takes great pains to correct those who pronounce the J. Taking Charlie's face in her hands, Janine kisses his wet cheeks, one then the other. "All better now?" She repeats the same couplet of kisses with Danielle and then Johnny. Only with Johnny she doubles the number. "Come, you need food?" She wears a pale green tunic, flowy silk pants, a white scarf around her neck, Isadora Duncan style. Her hair is swept up in a French twist. She never fails to make Nancy – who's wearing jeans, white blouse, black cardigan – feel frumpy.

"Bonjour, bonjour?" Janine says to Nancy, sans kiss. "What happened to the dessert?" Janine never calls Nancy by name because she has never forgiven Nancy for marrying her favourite son. Or this is what Nancy believes.

After washing off the bottom of her purse, Nancy hears Charlie calling "Mom" from the bathroom. He must need a wipe. If anybody had told her that children aren't fully potty trained until they're six, that she'd be wiping shit off bums six hundred times a year for eight years... She heads down a hallway hung with gray photos of Janine, the young ballerina, suspended in one nose-in-the-air pose after another.

"Let's try not to hit, okay?" she says as Charlie, sitting on the toilet, leans forward, head between his knees.

He makes a grunting sound, then starts counting backwards from twenty.

As much as she could use one, there is no glass of wine offered before dinner. Janine doesn't drink and Johnny's dad, Fred, has been drinking beer since eleven that morning though everyone's supposed to pretend he hasn't. Johnny never drinks at his parents' place because Janine would only fret about it.

Fred is already seated in the dining room at his place at the head of the table, smoking a cigarette. His full head of white hair is a sunny blond in the front, a nicotine job from chain-smoking while bent over his morning crossword puzzle.

Dinner is served five minutes after their arrival. The roast beef so rare it bleeds a circle around Nancy's rice, dying its base pinkish grey. Much to everyone's surprise, Johnny's younger brother shows up just as they've begun eating. Adam's sandy hair is roughed up in feathery tufts as if he's just rolled out of bed. One never knows whose.

The kids give him a boisterous, "Hi Uncle Adam."

Janine's eyes have narrowed and, with a flourish of hands, she says, "You didn't inform me you were coming?" She tells him to take off his jacket and hang it in the front closet. He keeps it on and sits down.

"Hey, Adam," Johnny grunts in the understated way they have together. Johnny and Adam have always been close, but their lives have taken such different turns that they no longer see each other very often.

Nancy smiles and lifts a hand. Fred doesn't acknowledge the late arrival because he's busy lifting a corner of his slab of meat and looking under it. Adam pulls a seat up beside Nancy, chairs are shuffled over, and Janine rises, muttering about fetching another table setting. Adam reaches across Nancy for the rolls. His jacket smells of dirt and pine, his breath of peppermint. Probably covering up a joint smoked on the drive over.

"I grew these steaks in my garden," announces Fred, grinning.

"You didn't, Grandpa," says Danielle, loving this worn-out game of his. "Steaks grow on cows."

Fred laughs too long and too loud, a strand of meat caught between his top and bottom teeth. The kids laugh with him and at him.

"Your grandchildren won't know what to believe?" chides Janine, plunking down fork, knife and napkin in front of Adam. "Best, perhaps, you should just not talk?"

Although Fred appears not to hear his wife, he's slurring when he speaks next. His former joviality now tainted with a child's rebellion.

"And I also grew the salad, and for you, Senator," he points at Charlie, "pickled beets. Eat 'em up and you'll grow hair on your chest."

"No," Charlie squawks, both thrilled and nervous that adults can be so silly.

"And on your back too," he adds and Janine sighs loudly.

Gardening is what Johnny's father took up after receiving a golden handshake at work six years ago. He was a gentle likeable drunk; early retirement satisfied everyone. He'd been a company man for too long to be fired and robbed of his full pension.

Danielle forks a beet into her mouth and chews with quick rabbit teeth. It makes a chattery, clicking sound. "Stop it," Nancy mouths, stern eyed, across the table to her daughter.

Danielle covers her mouth with two hands and keeps chattering, staring back belligerently. She knows Nancy won't yell at her at Grandmere's house. Much less smack her. Nancy takes a steadying breath. There are no bad children, some self-righteous mother once told her, just bad parenting. Ineffective, is what she is, totally ineffective.

"Pass the salt and pecker," says Fred, helplessly scanning the table.

Danielle and Charlie giggle and exchange looks. Janine makes a sound like spitting. "They are in front of your face?"

Nancy watches Johnny's eyes dart from parent to parent, absorbing every nuance of their mutual pain. She feels for him. Johnny is the one that holds the family together, the strained seam of a worn garment that long ago lost its shape. Now he'll make conversation with his mother to keep his father from speaking and angering her further. After this endless rosary of Sundays, Nancy knows the pattern well.

"Cougar scare in the neighbourhood yesterday. Did you read about it, Mom?" Johnny asks Janine. He doesn't wait for an answer, just keeps reeling her in. "One of those houses that back up on Mount Doug Park. An elderly woman was sitting there watching TV when she saw a cougar staring at her through the window. The woman scrambled out of her chair and the cat bared its teeth, swatted the glass, then disappeared."

"Truly?" Janine basks in his attention.

"At school the kids had to stay in at recess. Didn't you, Danielle?" Nancy offers.

Janine doesn't bother to turn her head in Nancy's direction.

"Yes, and I wanted to play pirates on the jungle gym," Danielle pouts, remembering.

Tired of eating, Charlie slips from his chair and under the table. Nancy expects Janine to give her the "please control your child" look but her gaze is fixed on her precious son.

"It's unusual to see one," continues Johnny. "The natives, you know, have always called them ghost cats because a sighting is that rare."

"I came up on a cougar once," Fred says grandly, gearing up for one of his stories.

"So how come we've never heard about it?" accuses Janine, putting her fork down with a cold clink against her plate.

"Never thought to tell it before." Fred dips to the right and steadies himself with a hand on the table.

"There's plenty you don't know about *moi*."

Under the table, Charlie begins quiet repetitions of his grandfather's crude French – "mwa, mwa, mwa." Nancy tries to nudge him quiet with a foot while Fred squints out the window to place the sound.

"Yes, so, what's the tall tale, Fred?" asks Janine.

"What?" asks Fred.

"Your story?" She wags her long, tapered nose. "About the cougar?"

"Oh, yeah, well," the energy drains from his voice. "Just that I almost ran over one in the boat. Was swimming between islands."

He says this so offhandedly Nancy believes him. Even Johnny and Adam check their father's face to see if this one might be true. Janine huffs, defeated.

"Anyone for more rice, salad? Danielle, there's more rice? Charlie? Boys? Where's Charlie gone?" She looks at Nancy.

"He's playing under the table."

Janine's eyebrows rise.

"Charlie," says Nancy adopting a scolding tone. Charlie doesn't answer. Ineffective.

"Come on out of there, big guy," says Johnny and Charlie's head pops up laughing into his father's lap.

Though others are still eating, Fred reaches for his cigarettes. Making an ashtray out of his half-eaten dinner, he taps his ashes over his plate and puts out the final sizzling butt in his rice. Then he gets up and disappears without a word, the sun still screaming daytime.

"Grampa goes to bed before me," says Charlie, back in his seat. He's seen his grampa do this forever and is being cheeky.

"He's up very early in the morning?" says Janine, staring down her grandson.

"Finish your meat, Sport, if you want dessert," says Johnny, coming to the rescue again.

JOHNNY WAS THE ONE who followed in his parents footsteps: well-paying job, married with kids, respectable home in the suburbs. Sometimes Nancy finds it hard to believe that she and Johnny once lived in an artists' co-op in Toronto's Queen Street West. It was where they met. She had fallen in love with pottery and dropped out of college in her sophomore year. Johnny, who had an undergrad degree in English, was the house poet. The poet and the potter. She hasn't thrown a pot since they moved west after becoming pregnant with Danielle, and Johnny's poetry's been redirected to writing public policy for the provincial government. A job Janine helped him land. The closest he comes to writing a poem are the rhyming treasure hunt clues he makes for the kids' birthday parties. Nancy often envies Adam who has, for the most part, resisted the grown-up world. Somewhere along the line he learned basic surveying and does just enough work to get by but mostly he's a dreamer, a rolling stone. Women float in and out of his life like smoke. He does what he wants to do, like gardening and jamming with his buddies. He lives on North Pender Island where he's bought a rough four acres and built his own small cabin. He rarely visits his parents. Johnny gives him a hard time about it but Nancy can't blame him.

"How's your garden?" she asks Adam, leaving Johnny and his mother to talk in low tones at the other end of the table. Adam hasn't shaved and the shadow of a beard looks good on him. Though Johnny is the better-looking brother, Adam has a certain Johnny Depp cool that she finds sexy.

"Chard made it through the winter, garlic's up, and I've got some transplants started. Broccoli, zucchini, cantaloupe, tomatoes. Still have some sweet cider if you want any."

"Sure, next time we're up for a crabbing expedition."

His flinty blue eyes linger absently on hers. Definitely stoned, thinks Nancy, smiling to herself. Adam doesn't drink, but smokes a lot of dope, which he plants amongst his pole beans and peas. Keeps the edges round, he once claimed with Peter Pan surety. He has a small runabout and the kids love to visit and help set his crab and shrimp traps, hauling them up every half hour to screech at anything trapped inside.

Something brushes against Nancy's bare leg. A pleasant chill trips up her spine. She glances at Adam, who's focused on cutting his meat. There's an inscrutable smile on his lips Nancy doesn't know how to take.

Cleaning up the kitchen, Nancy watches Johnny in the family room playing Lego with the kids. He's constructing "the castle of all castles, impenetrable to dragons, armies, and sorcerers' spells, due to small but effective antisorcery antennas placed at each corner of the roof."

He cuts a large donut shape out of cardboard for the castle's moat, which Danielle takes to the coffee table to colour with a blue crayon. She asks if he'll cut out the characters in his ongoing narrative – Dragon, Evil Sorcerer and Noble General – so she can colour them and tape them to chopsticks.

"Yes."

Though Nancy may take care of the kids' basic needs, Johnny satisfies their desires. Nightly, he reads to the kids or else makes up stories using the two of them as the central heroes. Every Friday he arrives home from a week's work with something to show for it, a surprise of some kind for the kids – pistachio nuts, a harmonica, newly-minted pennies. This past Friday it was a pomegranate and they'd all sucked on the seeds together and then had a spitting contest.

Charlie eggs his father on with questions.

"How strong is the general?"

"Stronger than Batman and Spiderman put together."

"How big is the dragon?"

"Twice as big as our house, with a temper ten times worse than Mommy's."

Johnny laughs but the kids don't. Nancy turns the faucet on, pretending she hasn't heard. Pretending it isn't true. She does not relate to that other her, that "Mommy" person.

Just yesterday that Mommy person had lost it with Charlie, who refused to put on socks before going next door to see the neighbour's new puppy. "Then you can't go," she said.

"Yes, I can," said Charlie.

"You'll ruin your shoes without socks."

"I hate socks."

"Come put on your socks." She had held them out.

"I'll wear Froggy boots." This was reasonable enough but she was determined to stick to her guns, knowing her kids will never listen to her if she doesn't follow through on her threats.

"I want you to wear socks with your boots then. Come here so I can put on your socks."

Charlie glowered at her and started to slip his bare feet into his Froggy boots. She'd snapped then, wrenched him off his feet and manhandled the socks onto his crying, squirming body, Charlie yelling, "I hate you," in his grating high-pitched voice. That night at bath time she noticed a big bruise on the pale flesh of his upper arm. She had kissed it, apologized to him, and prayed he wouldn't show Johnny.

"Does he breathe fire?" Charlie asks.

"Just smoke." Johnny laughs. "Like Grampa."

"Smoking's bad," proclaims Danielle as she starts to glue a line of small black triangles in the moat. "Look at my sharks."

NANCY HEARS THE RUMBLE of their Subaru pulling in the carport. Johnny's finally home from his poker night. The red numbers on the digital clock say 2:35. She listens for the time it takes for him to get out of the car and shut the door again. This is how she measures how much he's drunk. Johnny used only to drink in excess once maybe twice a year, on special occasions – New Year's, the year-end Old Timers' tournament. She never worried about it, considered it his catharsis, a stress releaser. This summer, Johnny's monthly poker night seems to have become a "special occasion."

Nancy maneuvers out from under Charlie, who had slipped into bed with her, robbing her of her few hours of freedom. She can feel the sting on her calf where his toenails scraped her in his sleep. She should carry him back to his own bed, she tells herself, before Johnny makes it upstairs. Like a large and friendly dog, two hundred pounds of carelessness could badly injure a small child. Johnny'd never forgive himself. She's left a glow of night lights to guide him, one in the stairwell, another in the hall, the bathroom and one to the side of the bed.

Charlie is big-boned, like Johnny, and already weighs close to fifty pounds. Nancy bends over and slips one arm under his knees, one under his arms and lifts. She feels something shift and click in her low back but grits her teeth and keeps moving.

As she crosses the hall she can hear Johnny fumbling in the fridge for a last beer. He won't find one. She hid them in the basement, behind the dryer, knowing that the sooner he's out of booze the sooner his private party will close down. As she lowers Charlie into his bed, a muscle spasm tears up her back. "What the..." She drops him with a thud onto the mattress and his eyes squint open.

"Go to sleep," she says with a warning finger. If he dares follow her back to bed, she swears she's going to lose it again. He starts to sit up and she shoves him back down, her back muscle cinching into a central throbbing knot. He whimpers and rolls over, yanks the covers over his head.

She closes her eyes. "I'm sorry."

She hobbles to the medicine cabinet, takes two muscle relaxers and returns to bed. Thirty-three years old with a bad back. Jesus fuck.

She hears Johnny's feet come heavy and arrhythmic up the stairs. Listens as he rounds the corner into the hall, then falls against the wall. The house shudders. There's the sound of glass breaking as the framed poem on the hallway wall, Johnny's first gift to her, falls off its nail. The light flares in the bathroom before piss tumbles into the toilet. He hasn't lifted the seat and she pictures Danielle sitting on the wet seat in the morning. He forgets to flush then turns on the tap, full force. A clatter of a toothbrush to the floor.

Nancy can't move now without pain. When Johnny comes and plops his weight onto his side of the bed, it jars her into momentary hell. He giggles as he takes off his socks.

"Nance, you wake. Got a goal for ya, sweet love. A beautiful thing. Roger rogered me the puck," he snickers, "from behind," another snicker, "up the boards and ha!, I flipped her over the masked man. Beauty shot, Nance. Jus' for you."

He wrestles free of his pants and falls back on the bed.

"Go to sleep, Johnny, it's late," she says, thinking how tomorrow was supposed to be her "day off." She has plans to go shopping, have lunch with a friend, maybe see a movie. Johnny won't be awake until two and then he'll be too hungover to be of any use. Unless she can get a sitter, which is doubtful, she'll be playing Candyland for the millionth time, cutting crusts off toast, breaking up fights...argh.

"Do ya love me, love me true, tell me and I'll get a goal for you," he rhymes.

"I love you, Johnny, but I'm tired and I pulled my back." She tries not to cry.

"Poor honey," he flops over on his side, "let me rub where it hurts." His arm thwacks clublike against her waist.

"Ow! No!"

"Ow!" Johnny echoes, slowly retracting his arm. "Sorry, Nance. I'm sorry, so sorry, I'm sorry. I got a goal for ya," comes his fading apology. There's an acidic smell on his breath as if something's fermenting in there. He rolls onto his back. "Always for you," he sighs. Twenty seconds later, he's asleep and snoring, his mouth slung open.

Nancy pictures his liver as a lump of deep red coral, parched and pocked full of holes. Like his father, Johnny's grandfather was also a drunk. Maybe the lineage went back further for all anyone knew. Johnny has assured Nancy he has forewarning on his side, and therefore choice. Choice, though, in her experience, is always more difficult than it sounds.

Mostly she believes they just need some time together. Just the two of them. Johnny away from his job, and she away from the kids. They need to make love under the stars, swim naked in a midnight lake, get stoned and spout bad haiku. It isn't too late to recapture those days. Or is it?

As Johnny begins a wet, sonorous snore, Nancy stuffs the pillow around her ears and feels the syrupy warmth of the painkillers start to kick in.

THE KIDS HAVE TALKED JOHNNY into going to Grammy and Grandpa's early this hot Labour Day Sunday so they can swim in their grandparents' pool.

Johnny is inside watching the hockey game with a half-lit Fred. Danielle and Charlie are playing tag in the pool's shallow end while Nancy, wearing one of her old bikinis, is stretched out on a poolside lounger. It's the first summer she's dared to wear a two piece and worries that her tan is actually accentuating instead of diminishing her stretch marks. She'd avoided stretch marks with Danielle, nightly rubbing vitamin E over her expanding gut, but was too tired to bother when pregnant with Charlie. She reaches for her O magazine. An ageless Oprah, on the cover, swirling in pink chiffon. "It's Never Too Late to

Reinvent Yourself" reads the bold yellow headline. Nancy studies Oprah's eyes for clues.

"Watch me!" Charlie yells in his squeaky voice, jarring Nancy from her thoughts.

She lifts her sunglassed face to watch him. He's wearing a bright orange life jacket and his arms flail inanely as he attempts to flip onto his back. She nods and returns to scan the magazine index.

"Watch this," he squeaks four seconds later.

Nancy waves a hand without looking up as she locates the page number of the article she wants to read.

At the pool's far end, Janine, who can never stop being "productive," at least whenever Nancy's around, is picking raspberries in Fred's garden.

"Are you keeping an eye on Charlie?" calls Janine over the fence.

Nancy waits to reply, seeing if it might force her mother-in-law to call her by name.

"I think Charlie needs a close eye?" Janine calls louder this time, her voice a rigid singsong.

"He's wearing a life jacket," Nancy replies while reading "letting go of one's habitual ways isn't easy but is often necessary in order to move forward."

"Then I could use a little help in the garden?"

Can't she stand to see anyone relax? Nancy reluctantly puts down her magazine.

"I'll be over in the garden with Grandmere," she tells the children.

As soon as Nancy's through the gate, Janine is handing her a bucket, jabbing the air with her index finger to the other side of the canes where she's picking.

"Only the ripe ones?" she says, as if Nancy's an idiot.

The ripest berries slip off with ease. Nancy eats every fourth or fifth berry, lifting her face to the sun and away from Janine.

"They will always choose the bottle over you, you know?" comes Janine's voice through the canes.

The raspberry on Nancy's tongue turns tasteless. What?

"Johnny is well aware of his tendency –" Nancy starts to say, feeling defensive. She refuses to be in the same boat as Janine. Ever.

"They will always choose the bottle over you?" Janine repeats, with more emphasis.

Nancy doesn't respond. It's an exercise in pointlessness to argue with this woman.

"He certainly does love those children, though?" Janine sighs loudly. "They might be his salvation?"

Nancy's gut churns. Is she implying Johnny loves his children but not her? That she would never be enough to keep him from becoming like his father? She pops another raspberry in her mouth without turning away. And another.

"Watch this," calls Danielle from the diving board.

Nancy peers over the fence, sees Janine's dark head watching three feet over. Her mother-in-law glances over and briefly catches Nancy eye as if to make sure she's been understood.

"Let's see Danielle, darling?" says Janine, her nose raised defiantly.

Danielle wiggles her tiny backside in preparation, two arms pointing downward like an elephant's kindergarten trunk, and drops into the water. When she surfaces and swims to the pool ladder, Janine waves a fist and cheers. Nancy gives her daughter the thumbs up sign.

"I did it!" Danielle yells. "I'm going to dive again." She scrambles up the ladder to trot back to the diving board.

"Look at me," Charlie shouts from the pool's other end.

Nancy squints at his tinny-sounding voice. He holds his nose and pushes his face into the water. Kicking his feet well below the surface, he travels a few inches ahead before popping up with a gasp.

Janine claps berry-stained hands up over her head.

"You're a real swimmer now," Nancy says.

"He's got a ways to go yet," mumbles Janine and disappears behind the canes.

JUST BEFORE THANKSGIVING, Fred is pulled over for drunk driving. Being his third violation, he loses his license for good.

Janine, who never learned to drive, insists that Johnny have Fred's car, a white Chevrolet, one of those nondescript American models with a tacky bourgeois name – *Celebrity*. Though ten years old, it's been used to drive to and from the liquor store and little else, and is in mint condition, Johnny doesn't want it at first, "an old person's car," he calls it. Nancy figures he doesn't like the thought of taking his father's seat behind the wheel. He's superstitious in that way. But their Subaru is going on two hundred thousand miles. They have a mortgage. They can't afford to turn down a free car.

The Cheverolet's velveteen upholstery is maroon and stinks of tobacco. "We'll get it cleaned," she tells him. They find a half-empty gin bottle stashed in the far corner of the trunk which Johnny decides to leave as a kind of souvenir. Or perhaps a challenge. They post an online ad for the Subaru and it sells within a week.

The Celebrity has power steering and brakes and surprisingly quick acceleration. Whenever Nancy drives it, just a gentle press of the pedal jolts the car into action, never failing to shock her to another level of mindfulness.

EVERY THANKSGIVING, the family gets together at Adam's place, taking the Pender ferry over early Sunday, staying overnight and leaving the next day after a late breakfast. Adam always prepares the dinner. Nancy is responsible for dessert — a couple of home-made pies and ice cream. Janine makes her homemade croissants for breakfast and brings the cocoa powder. This year, though, Fred refuses to go if he can't drive himself. Johnny offers to pick them up in Fred's car but that's not good enough for Fred. Janine insists he can't be left alone, that "you kids go on without us?"

"Your mother's such a martyr," Nancy says to Johnny.

"I don't know. Fred's pretty out of it. Probably burn down the house if she left him alone overnight."

"He could use a good scare."

Johnny stops and looks at her. "He's a good guy, Nance, just got a little lost along the way."

"I know," she apologizes, shaking her head. "Johnny, I don't make a good martyr."

He cups her face in his hands and kisses her. "I've been drinking too much. I know." He kisses her again. "It was a little phase, an experiment and it's over. I promise. Two drinks max from now on." He holds up a peace sign before his mouth slips under her hair to tongue her ear. She moans as shivers rise up like a crown on top of her head.

"Let's go away," she says. "A week, two. We both need a break."

"Maybe over Christmas?"

"Without the kids. Just us."

"Over Christmas?" He's incredulous. "Even if it wasn't Christmas, we can't leave the kids. Who would take care of them?"

"Your mom?"

Johnny looks at her. "She has to look after Fred."

"Then we'll pay someone."

"I couldn't trust them to a stranger for that long. They're too young yet."

"Your brother, then?"

"Mr. Responsibility. He'd probably lose them," he jokes.

He kisses her again but she turns her cheek.

ON THURSDAY, Johnny finds out he has to attend an emergency meeting on Saturday and another on Sunday, so he won't be going to Adam's either. Nancy figures they might as well cancel altogether and calls Adam.

"You can't leave me all alone on Thanksgiving," he protests over the phone. "Think of it as a holiday, Nance. Come kick off your shoes, I'll entertain the kids. Besides, I grew pumpkins this year and have a huge one for each of them."

The line about the shoes gets to her. That and the laid-back way Adam said it. The way he says everything. That tone had released her jaw muscles, muscles she hadn't even known were tensed.

"I'll make a pie and buy some croissants," she says.

"I've got cocoa."

She tells Johnny she'll bring home leftovers and they'll have a second Thanksgiving on Monday.

AFTER AN ENORMOUS DINNER meant for seven not four, games of hide-and-seek and several wrestling matches between the kids and their Uncle Adam, Nancy helps Danielle and Charlie into their pajamas before setting them up with a movie in Adam's king-sized bed. She guesses that Johnny's watching the football game at the pub but tries calling home anyway. At least, if he overindulges, he'll be dependent on cabs or a friend to get home, she thinks, since she has the car.

Adam has lit the leaning towers of candles that ring the deck floor. Thick curls of wax unfold from their sides and the flames flicker, sending out small messengers of light. It's mild for October, global warming waving its causal wand, and she and Adam are slumped in canvas recliners on his deck, army blankets over their legs. Like an old couple on a cruise ship, thinks Nancy, only they're surrounded by looming Douglas fir instead of ocean.

"Music," says Adam. "That's what we're missing."

He hops up and disappears inside. A minute later Norah Jones slides warm and easy from the bald-faced speaker positioned at the open door.

"God, I love this album," she says and takes a long sip of wine. "Johnny and I just don't take the time to listen to music anymore. I miss it." As Adam settles back in his recliner, she looks over to see the white sliver of a joint in his mouth.

"Come away with me," he says, the joint bobbing coolly between his lips.

"Yeah, that's my favourite song of hers," she answers, assuming this was what he meant.

Plucking a candle from the floor, he drags noisily on the joint then passes it to her. She hesitates.

"I don't know."

"Relax," Adam says in his kick-back voice. "It's late. The kids will fall asleep in my bed. Your work's over."

Your work's over. She repeats the words in her head three times, like Dorothy in *The Wizard of Oz*, leans her head back again and takes a long toke. Stars wink happily overhead. She knocks at her chest with a fist. "Ow." Takes a slug of wine.

They say nothing as they pass the joint back and forth, her thoughts gradually nudged aside by a sensation that her muscles are hunks of meat weighting her bones.

"How long did you nurse your kids for?" Adam says, popping the silence.

"Longer than I cared to," she answers, thinking it an odd question. "Johnny read somewhere that nursing for a least a year made for higher IQs. So the answer is a year and a day. Though I slipped in some formula when he wasn't watching. Why?"

"Lucky kids," he answers.

Confused, she lets go a bubble of laughter, enjoying the moment's sudden slipperiness.

"Mom brags that she nursed us for six weeks, just long enough to pull up her uterus." He pauses. "Now there's a gruesome image."

Nancy snorts out a giggle.

"Story has it that Johnny was a colicky baby. Is that the word? Colicky? It's hard to say. You kind of have to clear your throat when you say it."

Giggles seemed to be cuing up in Nancy's throat. "Charlie was too," she manages.

"She used to strap Johnny's bawling ass into a baby seat and put him on top of the dryer. She'd toss a handful of pennies inside then turn it on, go back upstairs and vacuum."

"This would calm him?"

"No, it was just to drown him out, so that she wouldn't have to listen to him crying. It was too painful for her."

Laughter is packing down into her chest like gunpowder. Though this part isn't really funny.

"He ended up with a herniated belly button."

"Terrible," Nancy articulates with some effort. She pictured Johnny's little pillow of a belly button and her voice scatters into jumpy laughter. This becomes hysterical stomach-grabbing laughter, soundless and open mouthed. Soon she's gasping for air, hiccupping to catch her breath and on the verge of crying.

"I'm not cut out for this mother stuff," she blurts, sniffing back tears. She feels instant relief in this confession. "I often think they'd be better off without me."

Adam doesn't say anything.

"Johnny's the one who wanted kids."

"He's always wanted kids."

"Yeah, too bad I'm not the one with the high-paying job. He should be the one who stays home. He's patient, he's fun, creative." She huffs out a laugh. "I don't even like them half the time. I lash out..." She presses her eyes with the heel of her hands, leans her head back.

"Kids are intense. There's no breaks. I can do it for a weekend and that's about it," says Adam.

"It's the no breaks, yeah." She's so grateful he understands. "I've turned into a bitch. A mean person. I never used to be..." she stops, tears threatening again.

"Not everyone's mother material. I mean, look at mine?"

She starts to laugh but it quickly turns to quietly crying behind her hands. Because Janine, Nancy believes, *is* a good mother. She loves her children. She never left bruises on their arms. She slides her hands to the top of her head and opens her eyes to the black sky. She feels disembodied, a gust of emotion whipping around in the dark. A warm hand, a human paperweight, is gently pressing on her chest. It's a relief to be pinned in her body again. Small seedlike kisses are being sown over the tops of her hands. The wetness of each planting cools afterward in the night air and is lost. When Adam's other hand slips to the exposed skin at her waist, she uncovers her eyes.

"You shouldn't be do −"

His mouth eats the rest of her less than effective sentence. His lips yield in the same soft way as Johnny's. He cups her face with both hands, something else Johnny does. She wonders if teenage brothers exchange information, or if the way one kisses is genetic. These familiarities are somehow confirming, comforting, but it's the differences that make it impossible to stop.

SATURDAY NIGHT and Johnny and Nancy have been invited to a party in the neighbourhood, a friend's fortieth. The couple has a son, so the kids are invited too. Charlie loves going to Max's because Max is two years older and has the latest Play Station and more games than Charlie knows what to do with. All day he keeps asking if it's time for the party yet.

"Not until dark," Nancy recites, until finally she turns on him and nearly screams, "If you ask me one more time, you'll be staying home." It's an idle threat because it's too late to get a sitter and Nancy really wants to go. An hour later, Charlie asks again. Infuriated, she grabs her startled son by the forearm and drags him to his room.

"Whaat?" he whines.

The fact that he forgot her threat only infuriates her further. She whips him by the arm into his room and he knocks his head on the corner of his dresser. She slams the door, breathing hard. As he starts to whimper in obvious pain, she scrunches up her face in regret, fists banging against her thighs.

THOUGH THE PARTY is only four blocks away, they take the car since it'll be late for the kids to walk back afterwards. And it's early November; the nights are turning cold.

A couple of oversized glasses of wine and Nancy's enjoying herself. The catered Thai food is delicious and there's a charismatic fellow, a professor of Asian studies, who's manically funny. Golden Oldies bounce from the speaker. The kids have remained downstairs for nearly three hours now, without bugging her once. She's almost forgotten she has kids. People have started dancing to what she remembers as "The

Shoop, Shoop Song." Johnny doesn't dance so she just watches them, lets her hips feel the beat. It isn't until nearly ten thirty that Charlie is tugging at her skirt, complaining that there's something in his eyes.

"You're sleepy," she says, hesitating to react to his outstretched arms. She sighs, puts down her glass and picks him up.

Downstairs she tells Danielle it's time to go but the kids are just beginning a game of Sardines and Danielle begs to stay.

"No, it's already past your bedtime."

"No, please. I'll come with Dad," Danielle offers as a solution, her eyes feverish with hope and fatigue.

Or I could stay and Johnny could leave, Nancy thinks bitterly. But in truth she's tired. Charlie had crawled into their bed in the middle of last night and she hadn't been able to get back to sleep. What with all the wine, she isn't going to last much longer.

Charlie starts wiggling out of her arms.

"I want to play too," he says, suddenly wide awake.

"We could both come with Dad," Danielle repeats. "Please."

Nancy sighs. She's doesn't have the energy to argue and knows she'll give in anyway. As usual. And she's guilty about losing it with Charlie earlier and wants to make it up to him. "Okay, but not for much long –" she starts to say, but Danielle and Charlie are already running over to the circle of kids.

"I'm GOING TO WALK HOME," Nancy says in Johnny's ear in order to be heard above the music. The party's just getting going but she suddenly likes the idea of having the house to herself. "I'm exhausted. Danielle and Charlie want to stay and come home with you."

"Sure, Nance, we won't be long," he says, pulls her in and presses his lips to the side of her head. Johnny has barely drunk at all since that last poker party binge. Tonight he's had his two beer max and his eyes are completely present. He holds a Sprite in his hand.

She thanks her hosts and leaves. Halfway down the driveway, she glances back at the house. Through the picture window, the birthday girl is waving a bottle of champagne in each hand. Johnny'll be fine, Nancy tells herself, turning her back.

She walks home along silent streets, moving in and out of the yellow pools of street lights then back into blackness. It's clear but cold and she puts on gloves, turns up her collar. As she rounds the corner, the street lamp in front of their house begins flickering like a strobe light. For three blinding seconds, it buzzes angrily at full brightness before going out completely. She stands in the dark until her eyes read-just, then walks up the driveway and inside. After a hot bath listening to the Norah Jones CD Adam burned for her, she rolls onto the mattress with a groan. With the house so perfectly quiet and still, she's asleep in a matter of minutes.

SHE'S WAKENED BY A SOUND like a shot, the walls quivering in its wake. The clock reads 1:21. Johnny is not in bed. She's up and downstairs, then outside, naked under a threadbare cotton nightgown.

The broken street light has resumed its mad flickering and Nancy feels part of a slow motion nightmare. She is unable to respond at proper speed; she sees and doesn't see Johnny walking in jagged circles apologizing to no one, his father's car a metal mouth clamped onto the base of the lamp pole. The neighbours are appearing in spills of light from their doors, putting on coats, hurrying forward. On the grass, pebbles of glass crunch under Nancy's bare feet, making tiny cuts she can't feel. Her breath makes little clouds in the air.

"Someone call an ambulance," she shouts. Then, no louder than a whisper, asks, "Where are the children?"

A man Nancy knows only by face finds Charlie under a hedge and rolls him gently out and onto the lawn. Charlie's unconscious, the skin on his face like bits of curled red ribbon. Nancy's arms are shaking so much she can't touch him, can only huff broken syllables in his ear.

"It's o kay Char lie. Help is com ing."

The man's wife comes over with a cloth that smells of rubbing alcohol. It'll sting, she thinks to herself, stepping away. Johnny's crying now, a big baby stumbling towards her in the blinking dark. His foot catches the curb and the tower of him falls to the ground and remains there. This isn't my life, she says to herself. This isn't my life, she repeats, tries on a smile.

Cranky Mrs. Moreland from next door finds Danielle behind the front seats. Apparently she was lying down in the back and was thrown to the floor. In a small, questioning voice, Danielle is calling for her dad. Not for me, thinks Nancy, crossing her arms against a creeping chill. She's not asking for me. Another voice, a man's, is saying something about her arm being hurt.

Nancy is unable to move from her crunchy patch of grass. She lifts her face up, to stare into the street light, which is now working fine. The world around her turns black.

CHARLIE IS WEEKS IN THE HOSPITAL, plus later surgeries to resolve the puzzle of his face. It will take months before he's able to smile without pain, until he can sleep through the night without waking and clawing her with crazy hands. Danielle wears a purple cast on her arm, which was broken in two places, and will undergo weeks of physio when it comes off. Though Johnny is remorseful beyond thought, Nancy has given him an ultimatum.

"One more drink and I'm gone. I'm only going to say it once."

Johnny can only nod in shameful agreement. "I promise you."

She needs to know if he can do it, will do it...not for her but for the kids. Because they need him, whole and forever. She, on the other hand, is utterly replaceable.

It's early April, the final Old Timers' tourney, when Johnny comes home with beer on his breath. He's not drunk, just spirited. "I had only two, Nance. Relax. It was a one-time thing."

Nancy doesn't say anything. Once again her threats have been ineffective. But this time, for the first time, she's following through.

Dear Mom,

Every day when I wake up I think you're still here, upstairs making coffee for Dad and dollar pancakes for me and Charlie. Dad makes pancake letters and spells our names. My D is hardest to make because the middle gets filled in.

We have a sitter after school. She is pretty nice and a really good drawer. Charlie's face looks better now. The little lines have turned white then the doctor says they'll disappear as new skin grows.

Daddy is taking us to Vancouver for Thanksgiving weekend. We are going to the Vancouver Aquarium and to Science World too. We are going to stay at a motel with a pool and a hot tub. We are going to Grandmere's on Sunday for turkey because Grampa won't go to Uncle Adam's. Will you have turkey where you are?

I have a times sheet to do or I can't watch TV, so I have to go.

Danielle

Nancy folds the letter and slips it amongst the others in an urn she made on her new potter's wheel. The urn has a raku glaze – a Japanese technique she's just beginning to master – and is one of her best pieces.

Acknowledgements:

I'D LIKE TO THANK JANICE MCCACHEN, CAROL Matthews, Laurel Bernard, Lucy Bashford and Patricia Young for their encouragement, editorial wisdoms and, moreover, their cherished friendship. Loving thanks for Bill for being brilliant and willing to share it. And thanks to the wondrous Fiction Bitches for their heartening feedback on "Medium Security."

Thanks to all the hard-working folks at Coteau Books, specifically Nik Burton for his twisted humour while holding my hot and cold hand. Thanks to my editor, J. Jill Robinson, for her hard work, insight and skillful guidance.

The following stories were previously published in literary journals: "Seers" – *Grain*; "Breaking Things" – *Room of One's Own*; "What Sort of Mother" as "Inviting Blindness" – *Dalhousie Review*; "Sunday Bastard" – *Antigonish Review*; "Raising Blood" – *Fiddlehead*.

Thanks to all those presses who continue to provide venues for new writers to test their mettle.

About the Author

DEDE CRANE is the author of the critically-acclaimed novel *Sympathy*, which was a finalist for the Victoria Butler Book Prize, and the teen novel *The 25 Pains of Kennedy Baines*. A second teen novel, *Poster Boy*, is forthcoming. Her first published story, "Seers," was a finalist for the CBC literary prize for fiction, and appeared in Grain magazine. She is also co-editor, along with author Lisa Moore, of *Birth, The Common Miracle*, a collection of non-fiction stories, due to be released in fall of 2008.

A former ballet dancer and choreographer, Dede Crane has studied Buddhist psychology at the Naropa Institute in Colorado and Psychokinetics at the Body-Mind Institute in Amherst, Massachusetts. She lives with writer Bill Gaston, and their four children, on the side of a mountain near Victoria, BC.

WWW.COTEAUBOOKS.COM